M. F. abbott

Many Cargoes

W. W. Jacobs wrote *Many Cargoes*, a selection of short stories, more than fifty years ago. Many of his writings were centred round the ports and water-ways of England. He himself spent his childhood on Thames-side watching the comings and goings of ships and their crews, and, because of this, was able to relate his tales with insight, feeling and humour.

This Red Lion Readers edition contains eighteen light-hearted tales about the various misadventures and catastrophes that befall captains and their crews, both on land and at sea. Frequently the captain finds himself in the embarrassing position of having to turn to his first mate and crew for assistance in disentangling himself from female ties unwisely formed. In 'Mated', Captain Evans is forced into this when he finds himself with one sweetheart on board his schooner, while on the way to visit another. His mate is more than ready to come to his aid, with a result more favourable to himself than to his master. Sometimes the crew are prepared to trade on their master's weaknesses, as in the case of the skipper of the *John Elliot*, whose belief in his abilities as a doctor is soon used by some of his lazy crew to their own advantage.

In *Many Cargoes* we see W. W. Jacobs' ability to portray a character in a few, well-chosen words: the sparring, sharp-tongued beauty who inevitably succumbs to the persistent suitor, the night-watchman weaving his incredible tales, the cabin-boy with his ingenious plans. He takes all these, and the sailors, sets them in ludicrous situations, and so produces very enjoyable reading.

RED LION READERS

General Editor:
A. R. B. Etherton, M.A., Ph.D.

Many Cargoes

W. W. JACOBS

CASSELL · LONDON

CASSELL & COMPANY LTD
35 Red Lion Square, London WC1
Melbourne, Sydney, Toronto
Johannesburg, Auckland

Set in 11 on 12 pt. Fournier type and printed in Great Britain
by Cox & Wyman Ltd., London, Fakenham and Reading

F. 967

Contents

Contents

A Change of Treatment

'YES, I've sailed under some crafty skippers in my time,' said the night-watchman at the wharf. 'Those that go down in big ships see the wonders of the deep, you know,' he added with a sudden chuckle, 'but the one I'm going to tell you about ought never to have been trusted out without his mother. A good many of my skippers had their fads but this one was the worst I ever sailed under.

'It was some years ago. I shipped on his barque, the *John Elliott*, as slow-going an old tub as ever I was aboard of, when I wasn't in a fit and proper state to know what I was doing. I hadn't been on her two days before I found out his hobby when I overheard a few remarks made by the second mate, who came up from dinner in a hurry to make them. "I don't mind saws and knives hung around the cabin," he said to the first mate, "but when a chap has a human hand alongside his plate, studying it while other people are at their food, it's more than a Christian man can stand."

'"That's nothing," said the first mate, who had sailed with the barque before. "He's half crazy on doctoring. We nearly had a mutiny aboard once when he wanted to hold a post-mortem on a man who fell from the mast-head. Wanted to see what the poor fellow died of."

'"I call it unwholesome," said the second mate very

savagely. "At breakfast he offered me a pill the size of a small marble. Quite put me off my food, it did."

'Of course, the skipper's fad soon got known for'ard. But I didn't think much about it until one day I saw old Dan'l Dennis sitting on a locker reading. Every now and then he'd shut the book, and look up, closing his eyes and moving his lips like a hen drinking, and then look down at the book again.

'"Why, Dan," I said, "what's up? You aren't learning lessons at your time of life?"

'"Yes, I am," said Dan very softly. "You might hear me say it. It's this one about heart disease."

'He handed over the book, which was full of details about all kinds of diseases, and winked at me hard.

'"Picked it up on a book-stall," he said. Then he shut his eyes and said his piece wonderfully well. It made me quite queer to listen to him. "That's how I feel," said he, when he'd finished. "Just strength enough to get to bed. Lend me a hand, Bill, and go and fetch the doctor."

'Then I saw his little game, but I wasn't going to run any risks, so I just casually mentioned to the cook that old Dan seemed rather queer, and went back to try to borrow the book being always fond of reading. Old Dan pretended he was too ill to hear what I said, and before I could take it away from him, the skipper came hurrying down with a bag in his hand.

'"What's the matter, my man?" said he. "What's the matter?"

'"I'm all right, sir," said old Dan, "except that I've fainted a few times."

'"Tell me exactly how you feel," said the skipper, feeling his pulse.

'Then old Dan said his piece over to him, and the skipper shook his head and looked very solemn.

'"How long have you been like this?" he said.

'"Four or five years, sir," said Dan. "It isn't anything serious, sir, is it?"

'"You lie quite still," said the skipper, putting a little trumpet thing to Dan's chest and then listening. "Um! There's serious mischief here, I'm afraid. The prognotice is very bad."

'"Prog what, sir?" said Dan, staring.

'"Prognotice," said the skipper; at least I think that's the word he said. "You keep perfectly still, and I'll go and mix you up a draught, and tell the cook to get some strong beef-tea on."

'"Well, the skipper had no sooner gone, than Cornish Harry, a great big lumbering chap of six feet two, went up to old Dan and said, "Gimme that book."

'"Go away," said Dan. "Don't come worrying me. You heard the skipper say how bad my prognotice was."

'"You lend me the book," said Harry, catching hold of him, "or else I'll bang you first and split to the skipper afterwards. I believe I'm a bit consumptive. Anyway, I'm going to see."

'He dragged the book away from the old man, and began to study. There were so many complaints in it, he was almost tempted to have something else instead of consumption, but he decided on that at last. He developed a cough that worried us all night long, and the next day, when the skipper came down to see Dan, he could hardly hear himself speak.

'"That's a nasty cough you've got, my man," he said, looking at Harry.

'"Oh, it's nothing, sir," said Harry in an offhand sort of way. "I've had it for months now off and on. I think it's perspiring at night that causes it."

'"What?" said the skipper. "Do you perspire at night?"

'"Never stop, sir," said Harry. "You could wring the clothes out. I suppose it's healthy for me, isn't it sir?"

'"Undo your shirt," said the skipper, going over to him and

sticking the trumpet against him. "Now take a deep breath. Don't cough."

'"I can't help it sir," said Harry. "It will come. Seems to tear me to pieces."

'"You get to bed at once," said the skipper, taking away the trumpet, and shaking his head. "It's a fortunate thing for you, my lad, that you're in skilled hands. With care, I believe I can pull you round. How does that medicine suit you, Dan?"

'"Beautifully, sir," said Dan. "It's wonderfully soothing. I slept like a new-born babe after it."

'"I'll send you some more," said the skipper. "You're not to get up mind, either of you."

'"All right, sir," said the two in very faint voices, and the skipper went away after telling us to be careful not to make a noise.

'We all thought it was a fine joke at first, but the airs those two chaps gave themselves was something sickening. Being in bed all day, they were naturally wakeful at night, and they used to call across the fo'c'sle inquiring after each other's health, and waking us other chaps up. And they'd swop beef-tea and jellies with each other, and Dan would try to coax a little port wine out of Harry, which he had to make blood with, but Harry would say he hadn't made enough that day, and he'd drink to the better health of old Dan's prognotice, and smack his lips until it drove us almost crazy to hear him.

'After these chaps had been ill two days, the other fellows began to put their heads together, being maddened by the smell of beef-tea and the like, and said they were going to be ill too, and both the invalids got into a fearful state of excitement.

'"You'll only spoil it for all of us," said Harry, "and you don't know what to have without the book."

'"It's all very well doing your work as well as our own," said one of the men. "It's our turn now. It's time you two got well."

'"*Well?*" said Harry. "*Well?* Why you silly ignorant chaps, we shan't never get well; people with our complaints never do. You ought to know that."

'"Well, I'll split then," said one of them.

'"You do!' said Harry. "You do, and I'll put a head on you that all the port wine and jellies in the world wouldn't cure. Besides, don't you think the skipper knows what's the matter with us?"

'Before the other chap could reply, the skipper himself came down, accompanied by the first mate, with a look on his face which made Harry give the deepest and hollowest cough he'd ever managed.

'"What they really want," said the skipper, turning to the mate, "is careful nursing."

'"I wish you'd let *me* nurse 'em," said the first mate. "Only ten minutes—I'd put 'em both on their legs, and running for their lives into the bargain, in ten minutes."

'"Hold your tongue, sir," said the skipper. "What you say is unfeeling, besides being an insult to me. Do you think I studied medicine all these years without knowing when a man's ill?"

'The first mate growled something and went on deck, and the skipper started examining them again. He said they were wonderfully patient lying in bed so long, and he had them wrapped up in bedclothes and carried on deck, so that the pure air could have a go at them. *We* had to do the carrying, and there they sat, breathing the pure air, and looking at the first mate out of the corners of their eyes. If they wanted anything from below, one of us had to go and fetch it, and by the time they were taken down to bed again, we all resolved to be taken ill too.

'Only two of them did it though, for Harry, who was a powerful, ugly-tempered chap, swore he'd do all sorts of dreadful things to us if we didn't keep well and hearty, and all except these two did. One of them, Mike Rafferty, took to his bed with a swelling on his ribs, which I knew myself he had had for fifteen years, and the other chap had paralysis. I never saw a man so really happy as the skipper was. He was up and down with his medicines and his instruments all day long, and used to make notes of the cases in a big pocket-book, and read them to the second mate at meal times.

'The fo'c'sle had been turned into a hospital for about a week, and I was on deck doing some odd job or other, when the cook came up to me pulling a face as long as a fiddle.

'"Nother invalid," he said. "First mate's gone stark, staring mad!"

'"Mad?" said I.

'"Yes," he said. "He's got a big basin in the galley, and he's laughing like a hyena and mixing bilge-water and ink, and paraffin and butter and soap and all sorts of things up together. The smell's enough to kill a man. I've had to come away."

'Curious-like, I just walked up to the galley and put my head in, and there was the mate as the cook said, smiling all over his face, and ladling some thick sticky stuff into a stone bottle.

'"How's the poor sufferers, sir?" he said, stepping out of the galley just as the skipper was going by.

'"They're very bad, but I hope for the best," said the skipper, looking at him hard. "I'm glad to see you've developed a little more feeling for them."

'"Yes, sir," said the mate. "I didn't think so at first, but I can see now that those chaps are all very ill. You'll excuse me saying it, but I don't quite approve of your treatment."

'I thought the skipper would have burst.

'"My treatment?" he said. "My treatment? What do you know about it?"

'"You're treating them wrong, sir," said the mate. "I have here" (patting the jar) "a remedy which would cure them all if you'd only let me try it."

'"Pooh!" said the skipper. "One medicine cure all diseases! The old story. What is it? Where'd you get it from?" he said.

6

"I brought the ingredients aboard with me," said the mate. "It's a wonderful medicine discovered by my grandmother, and if I might only try it I'd cure those poor fellows thoroughly."

"'Rubbish!' said the skipper.

"'Very well, sir,' said the mate, shrugging his shoulders. "Of course, if you won't let me, you won't. Still, I tell you that if you'd let me try, I'd cure them all in two days. That's a fair challenge."

'Well, they talked, and talked, and talked, until at last the skipper gave way and went down below with the mate, and told the chaps that they were to take the new medicine for two days, just to prove the mate was wrong.

"'Let poor old Dan try it first, sir,' said Harry, starting up and sniffing as the mate took the cork out. "He's been awful bad since you've been away."

"'Harry's worse than I am, sir,' said Dan. "It's only his kind heart that makes him say that."

"'It doesn't matter who is first,' said the mate, filling a tablespoon with it. "There's plenty for all. Now, Harry."

"'Take it,' said the skipper.

'Harry took it, and the fuss he made you'd have thought he was swallowing a football. It stuck all round his mouth, and he carried on so dreadfully that the other invalids were half sick before it came to their turn.

'By the time the other three had had theirs it was as good as a pantomime, and the mate corked the bottle up, and went and sat down on a locker while they tried to rinse their mouths out with the luxuries which had been given them.

"'How do you feel?' said the skipper.

"'I'm dying,' said Dan.

"'So am I,' said Harry. "I believe the mate's poisoned us."

'The skipper looked over at the mate very sternly and shook his head slowly.

'"It's all right," said the mate. "It's always like that for the first dozen or so doses."

'"Dozen or so doses!" said old Dan, in a far-away voice.

'"It has to be taken every twenty minutes," said the mate, pulling out his pipe and lighting it. The four men groaned all together.

'"I can't allow it," said the skipper. "I can't allow it. Men's lives mustn't be sacrificed for an experiment."

'"It isn't an experiment," said the mate very indignantly. "It's an old family medicine."

'"Well, they shan't have any more," said the skipper firmly.

'"Look here," said the mate. "If I kill any one of these men, I'll give you twenty pounds. Honour bright, I will."

'"Make it twenty-five," said the skipper, considering.

'"Very good," said the mate. "Twenty-five. I can't say any fairer than that, can I? It's about time for another dose now."

'He gave them another tablespoonful all round as the skipper left, and the chaps that weren't invalids nearly burst with joy. He wouldn't let them have anything to take the taste away, because he said it didn't give the medicine a chance, and he told the other chaps to remove the temptation, and you bet they did.

'After the fifth dose, the invalids began to get desperate, and when they heard they'd got to be woken every twenty minutes through the night to take the stuff, they sort of gave up. Old Dan said he felt a gentle glow stealing over him and strengthening him, and Harry said that it felt like a healing balm to his lungs. All of them agreed it was a wonderful sort of medicine, and after the sixth dose the man with paralysis dashed up on deck, and ran up the rigging like a cat. He sat there for hours spitting, and swore he'd brain anybody who interrupted him. After a little while Mike Rafferty went up and joined him, and if the first mate's ears didn't burn by reason

8

of the things those two poor sufferers said about him, they ought to have.

'They were all doing full work next day, and though, of course, the skipper saw how he had been deceived, he didn't mention it. Not in words, that is. But when a man tries to make four chaps do the work of eight, and hits them when they don't, it's an easy job to see where the shoe pinches.'

A Love Passage

THE mate was leaning against the side of the schooner, idly watching a few red-coated linesmen lounging on the Tower Quay. Careful mariners were getting out their side-lights, and careless lightermen were progressing by easy bumps from craft to craft on their way up the river. A tug, half burying itself in its own swell, rushed panting by, and a faint scream came from aboard an approaching skiff as it tossed in the wash.

'*Jessica* ahoy!' bawled a voice from the skiff as she came rapidly alongside.

The mate, roused from his reverie, mechanically caught the line and made it fast, moving with alacrity as he saw that the captain's daughter was one of the occupants. Before he had got over his surprise she was on deck with her boxes, and the captain was paying off the watermen.

'You've seen my daughter Hetty before, haven't you?' said the skipper. 'She's coming with us this trip. You'd better go down and make up her bed, Jack, in that spare bunk.'

'Ay, ay,' said the mate dutifully, moving off.

'Thank you, I'll do it myself,' said the scandalized Hetty, stepping forward hastily.

'As you please,' said the skipper, leading the way below. 'Let's have a light on, Jack.'

The mate struck a match on his boot, and lit the lamp.

'There's a few things in there that'll want moving,' said the skipper, as he opened the door. 'I don't know where we're going to keep the onions now, Jack.'

'We'll find a place for them,' said the mate confidently, as he drew out a sack and placed it on the table.

'I'm not going to sleep in there,' said the visitor decidedly, as she peered in. 'Ugh! there's a beetle. Ugh!'

'It's quite dead,' said the mate reassuringly. 'I've never seen a live beetle on this ship.'

'I want to go home,' said the girl. 'You've no business to make me come when I don't want to.'

'You should behave yourself then,' said her father magisterially. 'What about sheets, Jack; and pillows?'

The mate sat on the table, and, grasping his chin, pondered. Then as his gaze fell upon the pretty, indignant face of the passenger, he lost the thread of his ideas.

'She'll have to have some of my things for the present,' said the skipper.

'Why not,' said the mate, looking up again—'why not let her have your state-room?'

'Because I want it myself,' replied the other calmly.

The mate blushed for him, and, the girl leaving them to arrange matters as they pleased, the two men, by borrowing here and contriving there, made up the bunk. The girl was standing by the galley when they went on deck again, an object of curious and respectful admiration to the crew, who had come on board in the meantime. She stayed on deck until the air began to blow fresher in the wider reaches, and then, with a brief goodnight to her father, retired below.

'She made up her mind to come with us rather suddenly, didn't she?' inquired the mate after she had gone.

'She didn't make up her mind at all,' said the skipper; 'we did it for her, the wife and I. It's a plan on our part.'

'Come for her health?' suggested the mate.

'Well, the fact is,' said the skipper, 'it's like this, Jack; there's a friend of mine, a provision dealer with a good business, who wants to marry my girl, and the wife and I want him to marry her, so, of course, she wants to marry someone else. Her mother and I put our heads together and decided she should come away. When she's at home, instead of being out with Towson, directly her mother's back's turned she's out with that young sprig of a clerk.'

'Nice-looking young fellow, I suppose?' said the mate somewhat anxiously.

'Not a bit of it,' said the other firmly. 'Looks as though he had never had a good meal in his life. Now my friend Towson, he's all right; he's a man of about my own figure.'

'She'll marry the clerk,' said the mate, with conviction.

'I'll bet you she won't,' said the skipper. 'I'm an artful man, Jack, and, generally speaking, I get my own way. I couldn't live peaceably with my wife if it wasn't for management.'

The mate smiled safely in the darkness, the skipper's management consisting chiefly of slavish obedience.

'I've got a cabinet photograph of him for the cabin mantelpiece, Jack,' continued the wily father. 'He gave it to me on purpose. She'll see that when she won't see the clerk, and by and by she'll fall into our way of thinking. Anyway, she's going to stay here till she does.'

'You know your way about, cap'n,' said the mate, in pretended admiration.

The skipper laid his finger on his nose, and winked at the mainmast. 'There's few can show me the way, Jack,' he answered softly; 'very few. Now I want you to help me too; I want you to talk to her a great deal.'

'Ay, ay,' said the mate, winking at the mast in his turn.

'Admire the photograph on the mantelpiece,' said the skipper.

'I will,' said the other.

'Tell her about a lot of young girls you know who have

married young middle-aged men, and loved them more and more every day of their lives,' continued the skipper.

'Not another word,' said the mate. 'I know just what you want. She shan't marry the clerk if I can help it.'

The other turned and gripped him warmly by the hand. 'If ever you are a father yourself, Jack,' he said with emotion, 'I hope somebody'll stand by you as you're standing by me.'

The mate was relieved the next day when he saw the portrait of Towson. He stroked his moustache, and felt that he gained in good looks every time he glanced at it.

Breakfast finished, the skipper, who had been on deck all night, retired to his bunk. The mate went on deck and took charge, watching with great interest the movements of the passenger as she peered into the galley and hotly assailed the cook's method of washing up.

'Don't you like the sea?' he inquired politely, as she came and sat on the cabin skylight.

Miss Alsen shook her head dismally. 'I've got to like it,' she remarked.

'Your father was saying something to me about it,' said the mate guardedly.

'Did he tell the cook and the cabin-boy too?' inquired Miss Alsen, flushing somewhat. 'What did he tell you?'

'Told me about a man named Towson,' said the mate, becoming intent on the sails, 'and—another fellow.'

'I took a little notice of *him* just to spoil the other,' said the girl, 'not that I cared for him. I can't understand a girl caring for any man. Great, clumsy, ugly things.'

'You don't like him then?' said the mate.

'Of course not,' said the girl, tossing her head.

'And yet they've sent you to sea to get out of his way,' said the mate meditatively. 'Well, the best thing you can do ____'

His hardihood failed him at the pinch.

'Go on,' said the girl.

'Well, it's this way,' said the mate, coughing; 'they've sent you to sea to get you out of this fellow's way, so if you fall in love with somebody on the ship they'll send you home again.'

'So they will,' said the girl eagerly. 'I'll pretend to fall in love with that nice-looking sailor you call Harry. What a lark!'

'I shouldn't do that,' said the mate gravely.

'Why not?' said the girl.

' 'T'isn't discipline,' said the mate very firmly; 'it wouldn't do at all. He's before the mast.'

'Oh, I see,' remarked Miss Alsen, smiling scornfully.

'I only mean pretend, of course,' said the mate, colouring. 'Just to oblige you.'

'Of course,' said the girl calmly. 'Well, how are we to be in love?'

The mate flushed darkly. 'I don't know much about such things,' he said at length; 'but we'll have to look at each other, and all that sort of thing, you know.'

'I don't mind that,' said the girl.

'Then we'll get on by degrees,' said the other. 'I expect we shall both find it comes easier after a time.'

'Anything to get home again,' said the girl, rising and walking slowly away.

The mate began his part of the love-making at once, and, fixing a gaze of concentrated love on the object of his regard, nearly ran down a smack. As he had prognosticated, it came easy to him, and other well-marked symptoms, such as loss of appetite and a partiality for bright colours, developed during the day. Between breakfast and tea he washed five times, and raised the ire of the skipper to a dangerous pitch by using the ship's butter to remove tar from his fingers.

By ten o'clock that night he was far advanced in a profound melancholy. All the looking had been on his side, and, as he stood at the wheel keeping the schooner to her course, he felt a fellow feeling for the hapless Towson. His meditations were interrupted by a slight figure which emerged from the companion, and, after a moment's hesitation, came and took its old seat on the skylight.

'Calm and peaceful up here, isn't it?' said he, after waiting some time for her to speak. 'Stars are very bright tonight.'

'Don't talk to me,' said Miss Alsen snappishly. 'Why doesn't this nasty little ship keep still? I believe it's you making her jump about like this.'

'Me?' said the mate in amazement.

'Yes, with that wheel.'

'I can assure you——' began the mate.

'Yes, I knew you'd say so,' said the girl.

'Come and steer yourself,' said the mate; 'then you'll see.'

Much to his surprise she came, and, leaning limply against the wheel, put her little hands on the spokes, while the mate explained the mysteries of the compass. As he warmed with his subject he ventured to put his hands on the same spokes, and, gradually becoming more venturesome, boldly supported her with his arm every time the schooner gave a lurch.

'Thank you,' said Miss Alsen, coldly extricating herself, as the mate fancied another lurch coming. 'Good night.'

She retired to the cabin as a dark figure, which was manfully knuckling the last remnant of sleep from its eyelids, stood before the mate, chuckling softly.

'Clear night,' said the seaman, as he took the wheel in his great paws.

'Beastly,' said the mate absently, and, stifling a sigh, went below and turned in.

He lay awake for a few minutes, and then, well satisfied with the day's proceedings, turned over and fell asleep. He was pleased to discover, when he awoke, that the slight roll of the night before had disappeared, and that there was hardly any motion on the schooner. The passenger herself was already at the breakfast table.

'Cap'n's on deck, I s'pose?' said the mate, preparing to resume negotiations where they were broken off the night before. 'I hope you feel better than you did last night.'

'Yes, thank you,' said she.

'You'll make a good sailor in time,' said the mate.

'I hope not,' said Miss Alsen, who thought it time to quell a gleam of peculiar tenderness plainly apparent in the mate's eyes. 'I shouldn't like to be a sailor even if I were a man.'

'Why not?' inquired the other.

'I don't know,' said the girl meditatively; 'but sailors are generally such scrubby little men, aren't they?'

'*Scrubby?*' repeated the mate, in a dazed voice.

'I'd sooner be a soldier,' she continued; 'I like soldiers—they're so manly. I wish there was one here now.'

'What for?' inquired the mate, in the manner of a sulky schoolboy.

'If there was a man like that here now,' said Miss Alsen thoughtfully, 'I'd dare him to put mustard on old Towson's nose.'

'Do what?' inquired the astonished mate.

'Put mustard on old Towson's nose,' said Miss Alsen, glancing lightly from the cruet-stand to the portrait.

The infatuated man hesitated a moment, and then, reaching over to the cruet, took out the spoon, and with a pale determined face, indignantly daubed the classic features of the provision dealer. His indignation was not lessened by the behaviour of the temptress, who, instead of fawning upon him for his bravery, crammed her handkerchief to her mouth and giggled foolishly.

'Here's Father,' she said suddenly, as a step sounded above. 'Oh, you will be in trouble!'

She rose from her seat, and, standing aside to let her father pass, went on deck. The skipper sank on to a locker, and, raising the teapot, poured himself out a cup of tea. He had just raised it to his lips, when he saw something over the rim of it which made him put it down again untasted, and stare blankly at the mantelpiece.

'Who the—what the—who has done this?' he inquired in a strangulated voice, as he rose and regarded the portrait.

'I did,' said the mate.

'You did?' roared the other. 'You? What for?'

'I don't know,' said the mate awkwardly. 'Something seemed to come over me all of a sudden, and I felt as though I *must* do it.'

'But what for? Where's the sense in it?' said the skipper.

The mate shook his head sheepishly.

'But what did you want to do such a monkey-trick *for*?' roared the skipper.

'I don't know,' said the mate doggedly; 'but it's done, isn't it? It's no good talking about it.'

The skipper looked at him in wrathful perplexity. 'You'd better have advice when we get to port, Jack,' he said at length; 'the last few weeks I've noticed you've been a bit strange in your manner. You'd better go and show that head of yours to a doctor.'

The mate grunted, and went on deck for sympathy, but, finding Miss Alsen in a mood far removed from sentiment and not at all grateful, drew off whistling. Matters were in this state when the skipper appeared, wiping his mouth.

'I've put another portrait on the mantelpiece, Jack,' he said menacingly; 'it's the only other one I've got and I wish you to understand that if that only *smells* mustard, there'll be such a row in this ship that you won't be able to hear yourself speak for the noise.'

He moved off with dignity as his daughter, who had over-heard the remark, came sidling up to the mate and smiled on him agreeably.

'He's put another portrait there,' she said softly.

'You'll find the mustard-pot in the cruet,' said the mate coldly.

Miss Alsen turned and watched her father as he went forward, and then, to the mate's surprise, went below without another word. A prey to curiosity, but too proud to make any overture, he compromised matters by going and standing near the companion.

'Mate!' said a stealthy whisper at the foot of the ladder.

The mate gazed calmly out to sea.

'Jack!' said the girl again, in a lower whisper than before.

The mate went hot all over, and at once descended. He found Miss Alsen, her eyes sparkling, with the mustard-pot in her left hand and the spoon in her right, executing a war-dance in front of the second portrait.

'Don't do it,' said the mate, in alarm.

'Why not?' she inquired, going within an inch of it.

'He'll think it's me,' said the mate.

'That's why I called you down here,' said she; 'you don't think I wanted you, do you?'

'You put that spoon down,' said the mate, who was by no means desirous of another interview with the skipper.

'Shan't!' said Miss Alsen.

The mate sprang at her, but she dodged round the table. He leaned over, and, catching her by the left arm, drew her towards him; then, with her flushed, laughing face close to his, he forgot everything else, and kissed her.

'Oh!' said Hetty indignantly.

'Will you give it to me now?' said the mate, trembling at his boldness.

'Take it,' said she. She leaned across the table, and, as the mate advanced, dabbed viciously at him with the spoon. Then she suddenly dropped both articles on the table and moved away, as the mate, startled by a footstep at the door, turned a flushed visage, ornamented with three streaks of mustard, on to the dumbfounded skipper.

'Sakes alive!' said the astonished mariner, as soon as he could speak; 'if he hasn't put mustard on his own face now—

I've never heard of such a thing in all my life. Don't go near him Hetty. Jack!'

'Well,' said the mate, wiping his smarting face with his handkerchief.

'You've never been taken like this before?' queried the skipper anxiously.

'Of course not,' said the mortified mate.

'Don't you say of course not to me,' said the other warmly, 'after behaving like this. A strait-jacket's what you want. I'll go and see old Ben about it. He's got an uncle in an institution. You come up too, my girl.'

He went in search of Ben, oblivious of the fact that his daughter, instead of following him, came no farther than the door, where she stood and regarded her victim compassionately.

'I'm so sorry,' she said. 'Does it smart?'

'A little,' said the mate; 'don't you trouble about me.'

'You see what you get for behaving badly,' said Miss Alsen judicially.

'It's worth it,' said the mate, brightening.

'I'm afraid it'll blister,' said she. She crossed over to him, and putting her head on one side, eyed the traces wisely. 'Three marks,' she said.

'I only had one,' suggested the mate.

'One what?' inquired Hetty.

'Those,' said the mate.

In full view of the horrified skipper, who was cautiously peeping at the supposed lunatic through the skylight, he kissed her again.

'You can go away, Ben,' said the skipper huskily to the expert. 'D'you hear, you can go *away*, and not a word about this, mind.'

The expert went away grumbling, and the father, after another glance, which showed him his daughter nestling comfortably on the mate's right shoulder, stole away and brooded darkly over this crowning complication. An ordinary man would have run down and interrupted them; the master of the *Jessica* thought he could attain his ends more certainly by diplomacy, and so careful was his demeanour that the couple in the cabin had no idea that they had been observed – the mate listening calmly to a lecture on incipient idiocy which the skipper thought it advisable to bestow.

Until the midday meal on the day following he made no sign. If anything he was even more affable than usual, though his wrath rose at the glances which were being exchanged across the table.

'By the way, Jack,' he said at length, 'what's become of Kitty Loney?'

'Who?' inquired the mate. 'Who's Kitty Loney?'

It was now the skipper's turn to stare, and he did it admirably.

'Kitty Loney,' he said in surprise, 'the little girl you are going to marry.'

'Who are you getting at?' said the mate, going scarlet as he met the gaze opposite.

'I don't know what you mean,' said the skipper with dignity. 'I'm alluding to Kitty Loney, the little girl in the red hat and white feathers you introduced to me as your future wife.'

The mate sank back in his seat, and regarded him with open-mouthed, horrified astonishment.

'You don't mean to say you've thrown her over,' pursued the heartless skipper, 'after getting an advance from me to buy the ring with, too? Didn't you buy the ring with the money?'

'No,' said the mate, 'I—oh, no—of course—what on earth are you talking about?'

The skipper rose from his seat and regarded him sorrowfully but severely. 'I'm sorry, Jack,' he said stiffly, 'if I've said anything to annoy you, or anyway hurt your feelings. Of

20

course it's your business, not mine. Perhaps you'll say you never heard of Kitty Loney?'

'I do say so,' said the bewildered mate; 'I do say so.'

The skipper eyed him sternly, and without another word left the cabin. 'If she's like her mother,' he said to himself, chuckling as he went up the companion-ladder, 'I think that'll do.'

There was an awkward pause after his departure. 'I'm sure I don't know what you must think of me,' said the mate at length, 'but I don't know what your father's talking about.'

'I don't think anything,' said Hetty calmly. 'Pass the potatoes, please.'

'I suppose it's a joke of his,' said the mate, complying.

'And the salt,' said she; 'thank you.'

'But you don't believe it?' said the mate pathetically.

'Oh, don't be silly,' said the girl calmly, 'What does it matter whether I do or not?'

'It matters a great deal,' said the mate gloomily. 'It's life or death to me.'

'Oh, nonsense,' said Hetty. 'She won't know of your foolishness. I won't tell her.'

'I tell you,' said the mate desperately, 'there never was a Kitty Loney. What do you think of that?'

'I think you are very mean,' said the girl scornfully; 'don't talk to me any more please.'

'Just as you like,' said the mate, beginning to lose his temper.

He pushed his plate from him and departed, while the girl, angry and resentful, put the potatoes back as being too floury for consumption in the circumstances.

For the remainder of the passage she treated him with a politeness and good humour through which he strove in vain to break. To her surprise her father made no objection, at the end of the voyage, when she coaxingly suggested going back by train; and the mate, as they sat at dummy-whist on the evening before her departure, tried in vain to discuss the journey in an unconcerned fashion.

'It'll be a long journey,' said Hetty, who still liked him well enough to make him smart a bit. 'What's trumps?'

'You'll be all right,' said her father. 'Spades.'

He won for the third time that evening, and, feeling wonderfully well satisfied with the way in which he had played his cards generally, could not resist another gibe at the crestfallen mate.

'You'll have to give up playing cards and all that sort of thing when you're married, Jack,' said he.

'Ay, ay,' said the mate recklessly, 'Kitty doesn't like cards.'

'I thought there was no Kitty,' said the girl, looking up scornfully.

'She doesn't like cards,' repeated the mate. 'Lord, what a spree we had, cap'n, when we went to the Crystal Palace with her that night.'

'Ay, that we did,' said the skipper.

'Remember the roundabouts?' said the mate.

'I do,' said the skipper merrily. 'I'll never forget them.'

'You and that friend of hers, Bessie Watson, how you did go on!' continued the mate, in a sort of ecstasy.

The skipper stiffened suddenly in his chair. 'What on earth are you talking about?' he inquired gruffly.

'Bessie Watson,' said the mate, in tones of innocent surprise. 'Little girl in a blue hat with white feathers, and a blue frock, that came with us.'

'You're drunk,' said the skipper, grinding his teeth, as he saw the trap into which he had walked.

'Don't you remember when you two got lost, and Kitty and I were looking all over the place for you?' demanded the mate, still in the same tones of pleasant reminiscence.

He caught Hetty's eye, and noticed with a thrill that it beamed with soft and respectful admiration.

22

'You've been drinking,' repeated the skipper, breathing hard. 'How dare you talk like that in front of my daughter?'

'It's only right that I should know,' said Hetty, drawing herself up. 'I wonder what mother'll say to it all?'

'You say anything to your mother if you dare,' said the now maddened skipper. 'You know what *she* is. It's all the mate's nonsense.'

'I'm very sorry, cap'n,' said the mate, 'if I've said anything to annoy you, or anyway hurt your feelings. Of course it's your business, not mine. Perhaps you'll say you have never heard of Bessie Watson?'

'Mother shall hear of her,' said Hetty, while her helpless sire was struggling for breath.

'Perhaps you'll tell us who this Bessie Watson is, and where she lives?' he said at length.

'She lives with Kitty Loney,' said the mate simply.

The skipper rose, and his demeanour was so alarming that Hetty shrank instinctively to the mate for protection. In full view of his captain, the mate placed his arm about her waist, and in this position they confronted each other for some time in silence. Then Hetty looked up and spoke.

'I'm going home by water,' she said briefly.

The Captain's Exploit

IT was a wet, dreary night in that cheerless part of the great metropolis known as Wapping. The rain, which had been falling heavily for hours, still fell steadily on to the sloppy pavements and roads, and joining forces in the gutter, rushed impetuously to the nearest sewer. The two or three streets which had wedged themselves in between the docks and the river, and which, as a matter of fact, really comprise the beginning and end of Wapping, were deserted, except for a belated van crashing over the granite roads, or the chance form of a dock-labourer plodding doggedly along, with head bent in distaste for the rain, and hands sunk in trouser-pockets.

'Beastly night,' said Captain Bing, as he came out of the private bar of the Sailor's Friend, and, ignoring the presence of the step, took a little hurried run across the pavement. 'Not fit for a dog to be out in.'

Pulling up the collar of his rough pea-jacket, he stepped boldly out into the rain. Three or four minutes' walk brought him to a dark narrow passage, which ran between two houses to the waterside. By a slight tack to starboard at a critical moment he struck the channel safely, and followed it until it ended in a flight of old stone steps, half of which were under water.

'Where to?' inquired a man, starting up from a small pent-house formed of rough pieces of board.

'Schooner in the tier, *Smiling Jane*,' said the captain gruffly, as he stumbled clumsily into a boat and sat down in the stern. 'Why don't you have better seats in this boat?'

'They're there, if you'll look for them,' said the waterman, 'and you'll find them easier sitting than that bucket.'

'Why don't you put them where a man can see them?' inquired the captain, raising his voice a little.

The other opened his mouth to reply, but realizing that it would lead to a long and utterly futile argument, contented himself with asking his fare to trim the boat better; and pushing off from the steps, pulled strongly through the dark lumpy water.

'When I was a young man,' said the fare with severity, 'I could have pulled this boat across and back by now.'

'When you were a young man,' said the man at the oars, who had a local reputation as a wit, 'there weren't any boats, they were all Noah's arks then.'

'Stow your gab,' said the captain, after a pause of deep thought.

The other, whose besetting sin was certainly not loquacity, ejected a thin stream of tobacco-juice over the side, spat on his hands, and continued his laborious work until a crowd of dark shapes, surmounted by a network of rigging, loomed up before them.

'Now, which is your little barge?' he inquired, tugging strongly to maintain his position against the fast-flowing tide.

'*Smiling Jane*,' said his fare.

'Ah,' said the waterman, '*Smiling Jane*, is it? You sit there, cap'n, and I'll row round all their sterns while you strike matches and look at the names. We'll have quite a nice little evening.'

'There she is,' cried the captain, who was too muddled

to notice the sarcasm; 'there's the little beauty. Steady, my lad.'

He reached out his hand as he spoke, and as the boat jarred violently against a small schooner, seized a rope which hung over the side, and, swaying to and fro, fumbled in his pocket for the fare.

'Steady, old boy,' said the waterman affectionately. He had just received twopence-halfpenny and a shilling by mistake for threepence. 'Easy up the side. You aren't such a pretty figure as you where when your old woman made such a bad bargain.'

The captain paused in his climb, and poising himself on one foot, gingerly felt for his tormentor's head with the other. Not finding it, he flung his leg over the bulwark, and gained the deck of the vessel as the boat swung round with the tide and disappeared in the darkness.

'All turned in,' said the captain, gazing owlishly at the deserted deck. 'Well, there's a good hour and a half before we start; I'll turn in too.'

He walked slowly aft, and sliding back the companion hatch, descended into a small evil-smelling cabin, and stood feeling in the darkness for the matches. They were not to be found, and, growling profanely, he felt his way to the state-room, and turned in with all his clothes on.

'Time they were getting under way,' he said at length, and groping his way to the foot of the steps, he opened the door of what looked like a small pantry, but which was really the mate's boudoir.

'Jem,' said the captain gruffly.

There was no reply, and jumping to the conclusion that he was above, the captain tumbled up the steps and gained the deck, which, as far as he could see, was in the same deserted condition as when he left it. Anxious to get some idea of the time, he staggered to the side and looked over. The tide was almost at the turn, and the steady clank, clank of neighbouring windlasses showed that other craft were just getting under way. A barge, its red light turning the water to blood, with a huge wall of dark sail, passed noiselessly by, the indistinct figure of a man leaning skilfully upon the tiller.

As these various signs of life and activity obtruded themselves upon the skipper of the *Smiling Jane*, his wrath rose higher and higher as he looked around the wet, deserted deck of his own little craft. Then he walked forward and thrust his head down the forecastle hatchway.

As he expected, there was a complete sleeping chorus below; the deep satisfied snoring of half a dozen seamen, who, regardless of the tide and their captain's feelings, were slumbering sweetly, in blissful ignorance of all that the *Lancet* might say upon the twin subjects of overcrowding and ventilation.

'Below there, you lazy thieves!' roared the captain; 'tumble up, tumble up!'

The snores stopped. 'Ay, ay!' said a sleepy voice. 'What's the matter, master?'

'Matter!' repeated the other, choking violently. 'Aren't you going to sail tonight?'

'Tonight!' said another voice, in surprise. 'Why I thought we weren't going to sail till Wen'sday.'

Not trusting himself to reply, so careful was he of the morals of his men, the skipper went and leaned over the side and communed with the silent water. In an incredibly short space of time five or six indistinct figures pattered up on to the deck, and a minute or two later the harsh clank of the windlass echoed far and wide.

The captain took the wheel. A fat and very sleepy seaman put up the side-lights, and the little schooner, detaching itself by the aid of boat-hooks and fenders from the neighbouring craft, moved slowly down with the tide. The men, in response to the captain's fervent orders, climbed aloft, and sail after sail was spread to the gentle breeze.

'Hi! you there,' cried the captain to one of the men who stood near him, coiling up some loose line.

C

'Sir?' said the man.

'Where is the mate?'

'Man with red whiskers and pimply nose?' said the man interrogatively.

'That's him to a hair,' answered the other.

'Haven't seen him since he took me on at eleven,' said the man.

'How many new hands are there?'

'I believe we're all fresh,' was the reply. 'I don't believe some of them have ever smelt salt water before.'

'The mate's been at it again,' said the captain warmly, 'that's certain. He's done it before and been left behind. Those that can't stand drink, my man, shouldn't take it, remember that.'

'He said we weren't going to sail till Wen'sday,' remarked the man, who found the captain's attitude rather trying.

'He'll get sacked, that's what he'll get,' said the captain warmly. 'I'll report him as soon as I get ashore.'

The subject exhausted, the seaman returned to his work, and the captain continued steering in moody silence.

Slowly, slowly, darkness gave way to light. The different portions of the craft, instead of all being blurred into one, took upon themselves shape, and stood out wet and distinct in the cold grey of the breaking day. But the lighter it became, the harder the skipper stared and rubbed his eyes, and looked from the deck to the flat marshy shore, and from the shore back to the deck again.

'Here, come here,' he cried, beckoning to one of the crew.

'Yessir,' said the man advancing.

'There's something in one of my eyes,' faltered the skipper. 'I can't see straight; everything seems mixed up. Now, speaking deliberately and without any hurry, which side of the ship do you say the cook's galley's on?'

'Starboard,' said the man promptly, eyeing him with astonishment.

'Starboard,' repeated the other softly. 'He says starboard,

and that's what it seems to me. My lad, yesterday morning it was on the port side.'

The seaman received this astounding communication with calmness, but, as a slight concession to appearances, said 'Lor!'

'And the water-cask,' said the skipper; 'what colour is it?'

'Green,' said the man.

'Not white?' inquired the skipper, leaning heavily upon the wheel.

'Whitish-green,' said the man, who always believed in keeping in with his superior officers.

The captain swore at him.

By this time two or three of the crew who had overheard part of the conversation had collected aft, and now stood in a small wondering knot before their strange captain.

'My lads,' said the latter, moistening his dry lips with his tongue, 'I name no names—I don't know them yet—and I cast no suspicions, but somebody has been painting up and altering this craft, and twisting things about until a man would hardly know her. Now what's the little game?'

There was no answer, and the captain, who was seeing things clearer and clearer in the growing light, got paler and paler.

'I must be going crazy,' he muttered. 'Is this the *Smiling Jane*, or am I dreaming?'

'It isn't the *Smiling Jane*,' said one of the seamen; 'least-ways,' he added cautiously, 'it wasn't when I came aboard.'

'Not the *Smiling Jane*!' roared the skipper; 'what is it, then?'

'Why, the *Mary Ann*,' chorused the astonished crew.

'My lads,' faltered the agonized captain after a long pause. 'My lads——' He stopped and swallowed something in his throat. 'I've been and brought away the wrong ship,' he continued with an effort; 'that's what I've done. I must have been bewitched.'

'Well, who's having the little game now?' inquired a voice.

'Somebody else'll be sacked as well as the mate,' said another.

'We must take her back,' said the captain, raising his voice to drown these mutterings. 'Stand by there!'

The bewildered crew went to their posts, the captain gave his orders in a voice which had never been so subdued and mellow since it broke at the age of fourteen, and the *Mary Ann* took in sail, and, dropping her anchor, waited patiently for the turning of the tide.

The church bells in Wapping and Rotherhithe were just striking the hour of midday, though they were heard by few above the noisy din of workers on wharves and ships, as a short stout captain, and a mate with red whiskers and a pimply nose, stood up in a waterman's boat in the centre of the river, and gazed at each other in blank astonishment.

'She's gone, clean gone!' murmured the bewildered captain.

'Clean as a whistle,' said the mate. 'The new hands must have run away with her.'

Then the bereaved captain raised his voice, and pronounced a pathetic and beautiful eulogy upon the departed vessel, somewhat marred by an appendix in which he consigned the new hands, their heirs, and descendants, to everlasting perdition.

'Ahoy!' said the waterman, who was getting tired of the business, addressing a grimy-looking seaman hanging meditatively over the side of a schooner. 'Where's the *Mary Ann*?'

'Went away at half-past one this morning,' was the reply.

''Cos here's the cap'n and the mate,' said the waterman, indicating the forlorn couple with a bob of his head.

'My eyes!' said the man, 'I suppose the cook's in charge then. We were to have gone too, but our old man hasn't turned up.'

Quickly the news spread amongst the craft in the tier, and many and various were the suggestions shouted to the bewildered couple from the different decks. At last, just as the captain had ordered the waterman to return to the shore, he was startled by a loud cry from the mate.

'Look there!' he shouted.

The captain looked. Fifty or sixty yards away, a small shamefaced-looking schooner, so it appeared to his excited imagination, was slowly approaching them. Then a small boat put off to the buoy, and the *Mary Ann* was slowly warped into the place she had left ten hours before.

But while all this was going on, she was boarded by her captain and mate. They were met by Captain Bing, supported by *his* mate, who had hastily pushed off from the *Smiling Jane* to the assistance of his chief. In the two leading features before mentioned he was not unlike the mate of the *Mary Ann*, and much stress was laid upon this fact by the unfortunate Bing in his explanation. So much so, in fact, that both mates got restless; the skipper, who was a plain man, and given to calling a spade a spade, using the word 'pimply' with what seemed to them unnecessary iteration.

It is possible that the interview might have lasted for hours had not Bing suddenly changed his tactics and begun to throw out dark hints about standing a dinner ashore, and settling it over a friendly glass. The face of the *Mary Ann's* captain began to clear, and, as Bing proceeded from generalities to details, a soft smile played over his expressive features. It was reflected in the faces of the mates, who by these means showed clearly that they understood the table was to be laid for four.

At this happy turn of affairs Bing himself smiled, and a little while later a ship's boat containing four boon companions put off from the *Mary Ann* and made for the shore. Of what afterwards ensued there is no distinct record, beyond what may be gleaned from the fact that the quartette turned up at midnight arm-in-arm, and affectionately refused to be separated—even to enter the ship's boat, which was waiting for them. The sailors were at first rather nonplussed, but by dint of much coaxing and argument broke up the party, and rowing them to their respective vessels, put them carefully to bed.

Contraband of War

A SMALL but strong lamp was burning in the fo'c'sle of the schooner *Greyhound*, by the light of which a middle-aged seaman of sedate appearance sat crocheting a chair-back cover. Two other men were snoring with deep content in their bunks, while a small, bright-eyed boy sat up in his, reading adventurous fiction.

'Here comes old Dan,' said the man with the chair-cover warningly, as a pair of sea-boots appeared at the top of the companion-ladder; 'better not let him see you with that paper, Billee.'

The boy thrust it beneath his blankets, and, lying down, closed his eyes as the new-comer stepped on to the floor.

'All asleep?' inquired the latter.

The other man nodded, and Dan, without any further parley, crossed over to the sleepers and shook them roughly.

'Eh! what's the matter?' inquired the sleepers plaintively.

'Get up,' said Dan impressively, 'I want to speak to you. Something important.'

With sundry growls the men complied, and, thrusting their legs out of their bunks, rolled on to the locker, and sat crossly waiting for information.

'I want to do a poor chap a good turn,' said Dan, watching them narrowly out of his little black eyes, 'and I want you to help me; and the boy too. It's never too young to do good to your fellow-creatures, Billy.'

'I know it isn't,' said Billy, taking this as permission to join the group; 'I helped a drunken man home once when I was only ten years old, and when I was only——'

The speaker stopped, not because he had come to the end of his remarks, but because one of the seamen had passed his arm around his neck and was choking him.

'Go on,' said the man calmly; 'I've got him. Spit it out, Dan, and none of your sermonizing.'

'Well, it's like this, Joe,' said the old man; 'there's a poor chap, a young soldier from the depot here, and he's cut and run. He's been in hiding in a cottage up the road for two days, and he wants to get to London, and get honest work and employment, not shooting, and stabbing, and bayoneting——'

'Stow it,' said Joe impatiently.

'He daren't go to the railway station, and he daren't go outside in his uniform,' continued Dan. 'My heart bled for the poor young fellow, and I've promised to give him a little trip to London with us. The people he's staying with won't have him any longer. They've got only one bed, and directly he sees any soldiers coming he goes and gets into it, whether he's got his boots on or not.'

'Have you told the skipper?' inquired Joe sardonically.

'I won't deceive you, Joe, I have not,' replied the old man. 'He'll have to stay down here during the daytime and only come on deck at night when it's our watch. I told him what a lot of good-hearted chaps you were, and how——'

'How much is he going to give you?' inquired Joe impatiently.

'It's only fit and proper he should pay a little for the passage,' said Dan.

'How *much*?' demanded Joe, banging the little triangular table with his fist, and thereby causing the man with the chair-cover to drop a couple of stitches.

'Twenty-five shillings,' said old Dan reluctantly; 'and I'll spend the odd five shillings on you chaps when we get to Limehouse.'

'I don't want your money,' said Joe; 'there's an empty bunk he can have; and mind, you take all the responsibility—I won't have anything to do with it.'

'Thanks, Joe,' said the old man, with a sigh of relief; 'he's a nice young chap, you're sure to take to him. I'll go and give him the tip to come aboard at once.'

He ran up on deck again and whistled softly, and a figure, which had been hiding behind a pile of empties, came out, and, after looking cautiously around, dropped noiselessly on to the schooner's deck, and followed its protector below.

'Good evening, mates,' said the soldier, gazing curiously and anxiously round him as he deposited a bundle on the table, and laid his swagger cane beside it.

'What's your height?' inquired Joe abruptly. 'Seven foot?'

'No, only six foot four,' said the new arrival, modestly. 'I'm not proud of it. It's much easier for a small man to slip off than a big one.'

'It licks me,' said Joe thoughtfully, 'what they want them back for—I should think they'd be glad to get rid of them'— he paused a moment while politeness struggled with feeling, and added, 'skunks.'

'Perhaps I've a reason for being a skunk, perhaps I haven't,' reported Private Smith, as his face fell.

'This'll be your bunk,' interposed Dan hastily; 'put your things in there, and when you are in yourself you'll be as comfortable as an oyster in its shell.'

The visitor complied, and, first extracting from the bundle some tins of meat and a bottle of whisky, which he placed upon the table, nervously requested the honour of the present company to supper. With the exception of Joe, who churlishly climbed back into his bunk, the men complied, all agreeing that boys of Billy's age should be reared on strong teetotal principles.

Supper over, Private Smith and his protectors retired to their couches, where the former lay in much anxiety until two in the morning, when they got under way.

'It's all right, my lad,' said Dan, after the watch had been set, as he came and stood by the deserter's bunk; 'I've saved you—I've saved you for twenty-five shillings.'

'I wish it was more,' said Private Smith politely.

The old man sighed—and waited.

'I'm quite cleaned out, though,' continued the deserter, 'except for fivepence halfpenny. I shall have to risk going home in my uniform as it is.'

'Ah, you'll get there all right,' said Dan cheerfully; 'and when you get home no doubt you've got friends, and if it seems to you as you'd like to give a little more to those who assisted you in the hour of need, you won't be ungrateful, my lad, I know. You aren't the sort.'

With these words old Dan, patting him affectionately, retired, and the soldier lay trying to sleep in his narrow quarters until he was aroused by a grip on his arm.

'If you want a mouthful of fresh air you'd better come on deck now,' said the voice of Joe; 'it's my watch. You can get all the sleep you want during the daytime.'

Glad to escape from such stuffy quarters, Private Smith clambered out of his bunk and followed the other on deck. It was a fine clear night, and the schooner was going along under a light breeze; the seaman took the wheel, and, turning to his companion, abruptly inquired what he meant by deserting and worrying them with six foot four of underdone lobster.

'It's all through my girl,' said Private Smith meekly; 'first she jilted me, and made me join the army; now she's finished with the other fellow, and wrote to me to go back.'

'And now I suppose the other chap'll take your place in the

army,' said Joe. 'Why, a girl like that could fill a regiment if she liked. Pah! They'll nab you too, in that uniform, and you'll get six months, and have to finish your time as well.'

'It's more than likely,' said the soldier gloomily. 'I've got to tramp to Manchester in these clothes, as far as I can see.'

'What did you give old Dan all your money for?' inquired Joe.

'I was only thinking of getting away at first,' said Smith, 'and I had to take what was offered.'

'Well, I'll do what I can for you,' said the seaman. 'If you're in love, you aren't responsible for your actions. I remember the first time I got turned down. I went into a public-house bar, and smashed all the glass and bottles I could get at. I felt as though I must do something. If you were only shorter, I'd lend you some clothes.'

'You're a brick,' said the soldier gratefully.

'I haven't got any money I could lend you either,' said Joe. 'I never do have any somehow. But clothes you must have.'

He fell into deep thought, and cocked his eye aloft as though contemplating a cutting-out expedition on the sails, while the soldier, sitting on the side of the ship, waited hopefully for a miracle.

'You'd better get below again,' said Joe presently. 'There seems to be somebody moving below; and if the skipper sees you, you're done. He's a regular Tartar, and he's got a brother who's a sergeant-major in the army. He'd give you up directly if he spotted you.'

'I'm off,' said Smith; and with long, cat-like strides he disappeared swiftly below.

For two days all went well, and Dan was beginning to congratulate himself upon his little venture, when his peace of mind was rudely disturbed. The crew were down below, having their tea, when Billy, who had been to the galley for hot water, came down, white and scared.

'Look here,' he said nervously, 'I've not had anything to do with this chap being aboard, have I?'

'What's the matter?' inquired Dan quickly.

'It's all found out,' said Billy.

'*What?*' cried the crew simultaneously.

'Leastways, it will be,' said the youth, correcting himself. 'You'd better throw him overboard while you've got time. I heard the cap'n tell the mate he was coming down in the fo'c'sle tomorrow morning to look round. He's going to have it painted.'

'This,' said Dan, in the midst of a painful pause, 'this is what comes of helping a fellow-creature. What's to be done?'

'Tell the skipper the fo'c'sle don't want painting,' suggested Billy.

The agonized old seaman, carefully putting down his saucer of tea, cuffed his head spitefully.

'It's a smooth sea,' said he, looking at the perturbed countenance of Private Smith, 'and there's a lot of shipping about. If I were a deserter, sooner than be caught, I would slip overboard tonight with a lifebelt and take my chance.'

'I wouldn't,' said Mr Smith, with much decision.

'You wouldn't? Not if you were quite near another ship?' cooed Dan.

'Not if I was near fifty ships, all trying to see which could pick me up first,' replied Mr Smith, with some heat.

'Then we shall have to leave you to your fate,' said Dan solemnly. 'If a man's unreasonable, his best friends can do nothing for him.'

'Throw all his clothes overboard, anyway,' said Billy.

'That's a good idea of the boy's. You leave his ears alone,' said Joe, stopping the ready hand of the exasperated Dan. 'He's got more sense than any of us. Can you think of anything else, Billy? What shall we do then?'

The eyes of all were turned upon their youthful deliverer,

those of Mr Smith being painfully prominent. It was a proud moment for Billy, and he sat silent for some time, with a look of ineffable wisdom and thought upon his face. At length he spoke.

'Let somebody else have a turn,' he said generously.

The voice of the crochet worker broke the silence.

'Paint him all over with stripes of different coloured paint, and let him pretend he's mad, and didn't know how he got here,' he said, with an uncontrollable ring of pride at the idea, which was very coldly received, Private Smith being noticeably hard on it.

'I know,' said Billy shrilly, clapping his hands. 'I've got it. I've got it. After he's thrown his clothes overboard tonight, let him go overboard too, with a line.'

'And tow him the rest of the way, and throw biscuits to him, I suppose,' snarled Dan.

'No,' said the youthful genius scornfully; 'pretend he's been upset from a boat, and has been swimming about, and we heard him cry out for help and rescued him.'

'It's about the best way out of it,' said Joe, after some deliberation; 'it's warm weather, and you won't take any harm, mate. Do it in my watch, and I'll pull you out directly.'

'Wouldn't it do if you just threw a bucket of water over me and *said* you'd pulled me out?' suggested the victim. 'The other thing seems a downright *lie*.'

'No,' said Billy authoritatively, 'you've got to look half-drowned, and swallow a lot of water, and your eyes be all bloodshot.'

Everybody being eager for the adventure, except Private Smith, the arrangements were at once concluded, and the approach of night impatiently awaited. It was just before midnight when Smith, who had forgotten for the time his troubles in sleep, was shaken into wakefulness.

'Cold water, sir?' said Billy gleefully.

In no mood for frivolity, Private Smith rose and followed

the youth on deck. The air struck him as chill as he stood there; but, for all that, it was with a sense of relief that he saw Her Majesty's uniform go over the side and sink into the dark water.

'He doesn't look much with his padding off, does he?' said Billy, who had been eyeing him critically.

'You go below,' said Dan sharply.

'Garn,' said Billy indignantly; 'I want to see the fun as well as you do. I thought of it.'

'Fun?' said the old man severely. 'Fun? To see a fellow creature suffering, and perhaps drowned.'

'I don't think I had better go,' said the victim; 'it seems rather underhand.'

'Yes you will,' said Joe. 'Wind this line round and round your arm, and just swim gently till I pull you in.'

Sorely against his inclination Private Smith took hold of the line, and, hanging over the side of the schooner, felt the temperature with his foot, and, slowly and tenderly, with many little gasps, commited his body to the deep. Joe paid out the line and waited, letting out more line, when the man in the water, who was getting anxious, started to come in hand over hand.

'That'll do,' said Dan at length.

'I think it will,' said Joe, and, putting his hand to his mouth, gave a mighty shout. It was answered almost directly by startled roars from the cabin, and the skipper and mate came rushing hastily upon deck, to see the crew, in their sleeping gear, forming an excited group round Joe, and peering eagerly over the side.

'What's the matter?' demanded the skipper.

'Somebody in the water, sir,' said Joe, relinquishing the wheel to one of the other seamen, and hauling in the line. 'I heard a cry from the water and threw a line, and, by gum, I've hooked it!'

He hauled in, lustily aided by the skipper, until the long

white body of Private Smith, blanched with the cold, came bumping against the schooner's side.

'It's a mermaid,' said the mate, who was inclined to be superstitious, as he peered doubtfully down at it. 'Let it go, Joe.'

'Haul it in, boys,' said the skipper impatiently; and two of the men clambered over the side and, stooping down, raised it from the water.

In the midst of a puddle, which he brought with him, Private Smith was laid on the deck, and, waving his arms about, fought wildly for his breath.

'Fetch one of those empties,' said the skipper quickly, as he pointed to some barrels ranged along the side.

The men rolled one over, and then aided the skipper in placing the long fair form of their visitor across it, and to trundle it lustily up and down the deck, his legs forming convenient handles for the energetic operators.

'He's coming round,' said the mate, checking them; 'he's speaking. How do you feel, my poor fellow?'

He put his ear down, but the action was unnecessary. Private Smith felt bad, and, in the plainest English he could think of at the moment, said so distinctly.

'He's swearing,' said the mate. 'He ought to be ashamed of himself.'

'Yes,' said the skipper austerely; 'and him so near death too. How did you get in the water?'

'Went for a swim,' panted Smith surlily.

'*Swim?*' echoed the skipper. 'Why, we're ten miles from land!'

'His mind's wandering, poor fellow,' interrupted Joe hurriedly. 'What boat did you fall out of, matey?'

'A row-boat,' said Smith, trying to roll out of reach of the skipper, who was down on his knees flaying him alive with a roller-towel. 'I had to undress in the water to keep afloat. I've lost all my clothes.'

'Poor fellow,' said Dan.

'A gold watch and chain, my purse, and three of the nicest fellows that ever breathed,' continued Smith, who was now entering into the spirit of the thing.

'Poor chaps,' said the skipper solemnly. 'Any of them leave any family?'

'Four,' said Smith sadly.

'Children?' queried the mate.

'Families,' said Smith.

'Look here,' said the mate, but the watchful Joe interrupted him.

'His mind's wandering,' he said hastily. 'He can't count, poor chap. We'd better get him to bed.'

'Ah, do,' said the skipper, and, assisted by his friends, the rescued man was half led, half carried below and put between the blankets, where he lay luxuriously sipping a glass of brandy and water, sent from the cabin.

'How'd I do it?' he inquired, with a satisfied air.

'There was no need to tell all those lies about it,' said Dan sharply; 'instead of one little lie you told half a dozen. I don't want anything more to do with you. You start afresh now, like a new-born babe.'

'All right,' said Smith shortly; and, being very much fatigued with his exertions, and much refreshed by the brandy, fell into a deep and peaceful sleep.

The morning was well advanced when he awoke, and the fo'c'sle empty except for the faithful Joe, who was standing by his side, with a heap of clothing under his arm.

'Try these on,' said he, as Smith stared at him half awake; 'they'll be better than nothing, at any rate.'

The soldier leaped from his bunk and gratefully proceeded to dress himself, Joe eyeing him critically as the trousers climbed up his long legs, and the sleeves of the jacket did their best to conceal his elbows.

'What do I look like?' he inquired anxiously, as he finished.

'Six foot and a half of misery,' piped the shrill voice of Billy promptly, as he thrust his head in at the fo'c'sle. 'You can't go to church in those clothes.'

'Well, they'll do for the ship, but you can't go ashore in them,' said Joe, as he edged towards the ladder, and suddenly sprang up a step or two to let fly at the boy.

'The old man wants to see you; be careful what you say to him.'

With a very unsuccessful attempt to appear unconscious of the figure he cut, Smith went up on deck for the interview.

'We can't do anything until we get to London,' said the skipper, as he made copious notes of Smith's adventures. 'As soon as we get there, I'll lend you the money to telegraph your friends to tell them you're safe and to send you some clothes, and of course you'll have free board and lodging till it comes, and I'll write out an account of it for the newspapers.'

'You're very good,' said Smith blankly.

'And I don't know what you are,' said the skipper, interrogatively; 'but you ought to go in for swimming as a profession—six hours' swimming about like that is wonderful.'

'You don't know what you can do till you have to,' said Smith modestly, as he backed slowly away; 'but I never want to see the water again as long as I live.'

The two remaining days of their passage passed all too quickly for the men, who were casting about for some way out of the difficulty which they foresaw would arise when they reached London.

'If you'd only got decent clothes,' said Joe, as they passed Gravesend, 'you could go off and send a telegram, and not come back; but you couldn't go five yards in those things without having a crowd after you.'

'I shall have to be taken I suppose,' said Smith moodily.

'And poor old Dan'll get six months hard for helping you off,' said Joe sympathetically, as a bright idea occurred to him.

'Rubbish!' said Dan uneasily. 'He can stick to his tale of being upset; anyway, the skipper saw him pulled out of the water. He's too honest a chap to get an old man into trouble for trying to help him.'

'He must have a new rig-out, Dan,' said Joe softly. 'You and I will go and buy it. I'll do the choosing, and you'll do the paying. Why, it'll be a regular treat for you to lay out a little money, Dan. We'll have quite an evening's shopping, everything of the best.'

The infuriated Dan gasped for breath, and looked helplessly at the grinning crew.

'I'll see him—overboard first,' he said furiously.

'Please yourself,' said Joe, shortly. 'If he's caught you'll get six months. As it is, you've got a chance to do a nice, kind little Christian act, because, of course, that twenty-five bob you got out of him won't anything like pay for his toggery.'

Almost beside himself with indignation, the old man moved off, and said not another word until they were made fast to the wharf at Limehouse. He did not even break silence when Joe, taking him affectionately by the arm, led him aft to the skipper.

'Dan and I, sir,' said Joe very respectfully, 'would like to go ashore for a little shopping. Dan has very kindly offered to lend that poor chap the money for some clothes, and he wants me to go with him to help carry them.'

'Ay, ay,' said the skipper, with a benevolent smile at the aged philanthropist. 'You'd better go at once, before the shops shut.'

'We'll run, sir,' said Joe, and taking Dan by the arm, dragged him into the street at a trot.

Nearly a couple of hours passed before they returned, and no child watched with greater eagerness the opening of a birthday present than Smith watched the undoing of the numerous parcels with which they were laden.

'He's a regular fairy godmother, isn't he?' said Joe, as

Smith joyously dressed himself in a very presentable tweed suit, serviceable boots, and a bowler hat. 'We had a dreadful job to get a suit big enough, and the only one we could get was rather more money than we wanted to give, wasn't it, Dan?'

The fairy godmother strove manfully with his feelings.

'You'll do now,' said Joe. 'I haven't got much, but what I have you're welcome to.' He put his hand into his pocket and pulled out some loose coins. 'What have you got, mates?'

With decent goodwill the other men turned out their pockets, and, adding to the store, heartily pressed it upon the reluctant Smith, who, after shaking hands gratefully, followed Joe on deck.

'You've got enough to pay your fare,' said the latter; 'and I've told the skipper you are going ashore to send off telegrams. If you send the money back to Dan, I'll never forgive you.'

'I won't then,' said Smith firmly; 'but I'll send theirs back to the other chaps. Goodbye.'

Joe shook him by the hand again, and bade him go while the coast was clear, advice which Smith hastened to follow, though he turned and looked back to wave his hand to the crew, who had come up on deck silently to see him off; all but the philanthropist, who was down below with a stump of lead-pencil and a piece of paper doing sums.

The Skipper of the *Osprey*

IT was a quarter to six in the morning as the mate of the sailing-barge *Osprey* came on deck and looked round for the master, who had been sleeping ashore and was somewhat overdue. Ten minutes passed before he appeared on the wharf, and the mate saw with surprise that he was leaning on the arm of a pretty girl of twenty, as he hobbled painfully down to the barge.

'Here you are then,' said the mate, his face clearing. 'I began to think you weren't coming.'

'I'm not,' said the skipper; 'I've got the gout cruel badly. My daughter here's going to take my place, and I'm going to take it easy in bed for a bit.'

'I'll go and make it for you,' said the mate.

'I mean my bed at home,' said the skipper sharply. 'I want good nursing and attention.'

The mate looked puzzled.

'But you don't really mean to say this young lady is coming aboard instead of you?' he said.

'That's just what I do mean,' said the skipper. 'She knows as much about it as I do. She lived aboard with me until she was quite a big girl. You'll take your orders from her. What are you whistling about? Can't I do as I like about my own ship?'

46

'Of course you can,' said the mate dryly; 'and I suppose I can whistle if I like—I've never heard any orders against it.'

'Give me a kiss, Meg, and get aboard,' said the skipper, leaning on his stick and turning his cheek to his daughter, who obediently gave him a perfunctory kiss on the left eyebrow, and sprang lightly aboard the barge.

'Cast off,' said she, in a business-like manner, as she seized a boat-hook and pushed off from the jetty. 'Bye-bye, Dad, and go straight home, mind; the cab's waiting.'

'Ay, ay, my dear,' said the proud father, his eye moistening with paternal pride as his daughter, throwing off her jacket, ran and assisted the mate with the sail. 'What a fine boy she would have made.'

He watched the barge until she was well under way, and then, waving his hand to his daughter, crawled slowly back to the cab; and, being to a certain extent a believer in homoeopathy, treated his complaint with a glass of rum.

'I'm sorry your father's so bad, miss,' said the mate, who was still somewhat dazed by the recent proceedings, as the girl came up and took the wheel from him. 'He was complaining a good bit all the way up.'

'A wilful man must have his way,' said Miss Cringle, with a shake of her head. 'It's no good me saying anything, because directly my back's turned he has his own way again.'

The mate shook his head despondently.

'You'd better get your bedding up and make your arrangements forward,' said the new skipper presently. There was a look of indulgent admiration in the mate's eye, and she thought it necessary to check it.

'All right,' said the other, 'plenty of time for that; the river's a bit thick just now.'

'What do you mean?' inquired the girl hastily.

'Some of these things are not as careful as they might be,' said the mate, noting the ominous sparkle of her eye, 'and they might scrape the paint off.'

'Look here, my lad,' said the new skipper grimly, 'if you think you can steer better than me, you'd better keep it to yourself, that's all. Now suppose you see about your bedding, as I said.'

The mate went, albeit he was rather surprised at himself for doing so, and hid his annoyance and confusion beneath the mattress which he brought up on his head. His job completed, he came aft again, and sitting on the hatches, lit his pipe.

'This is just the weather for a pleasant cruise,' he said amiably, after a few whiffs. 'You've chosen a nice time for it.'

'I don't mind the weather,' said the girl, who fancied that there was a little latent sarcasm somewhere. 'I think you'd better wash the decks now.'

'Washed them last night,' said the mate, without moving.

'Ah, after dark, perhaps,' said the girl. 'Well, I think I'll have them done again.'

The mate sat pondering rebelliously for a few minutes, then he removed his jacket, put on in honour of the new skipper, and, fetching the bucket and mop, silently obeyed orders.

'You seem to be very fond of sitting down,' remarked the girl, after he had finished; 'can't you find something else to do?'

'I don't know,' replied the mate slowly; 'I thought you were looking after that.'

The girl bit her lip, and was looking carefully around her, when they were both disturbed by the unseemly behaviour of the master of a passing craft.

'Jack!' he yelled in a tone of strong amazement, 'Jack!'

'Halloa!' cried the mate.

'Why didn't you tell us?' yelled the other reproachfully.

'Tell you what?' roared the mystified mate.

The master of the other craft, holding on to the stays with

48

one hand, jerked his thumb expressively towards Miss Cringle, and waited.

'When was it?' he screamed anxiously, as he realized that his craft was rapidly carrying him out of earshot.

The mate smiled feebly, and glanced uneasily at the girl, who, with a fine colour and an air of vast unconcern, was looking straight in front of her; and it was a relief to both of them when they found themselves hesitating and dodging in front of a schooner which was coming up.

'Do you want all the river?' demanded the exasperated master of the latter vessel, running to the side as they passed.

'Perhaps you'd better let me take the wheel a bit,' said the mate, not without a little malice in his voice.

'No; you can go and keep a look-out in the bows,' said the girl serenely. 'It'll prevent misunderstandings, too. Better take the potatoes with you and peel them for dinner.'

The mate complied, and the voyage proceeded in silence, the steering being rendered a little nicer than usual by various nautical sparks bringing their boats a bit closer than was necessary in order to obtain a good view of the fair steersman.

After dinner, the tide having turned and a stiff headwind blowing, they brought up off Sheppey. It began to rain hard, and the crew of the *Osprey*, having made all snug above, retired to the cabin to resume their quarrel.

'Don't mind me,' said Miss Cringle scathingly, as the mate lit his pipe.

'Well, I didn't think you minded,' replied the mate; 'the old man——'

'Who?' interrupted Miss Cringle, in a tone of polite inquiry.

'Captain Cringle,' said the mate, correcting himself, 'smokes a great deal, and I've heard him say that you liked the smell of it.'

'There's pipes and pipes,' said Miss Cringle oracularly.

The mate flung his on the floor and crunched it beneath his

heel, then he thrust his hands in his pockets, and, leaning back, scowled darkly up at the rain as it crackled on the skylight.

'If you are going to show off your nasty temper,' said the girl severely, 'you'd better go forward. It's not quite the thing after all for you to be down here—not that I study appearances much.'

'I shouldn't think you did,' retorted the mate, whose temper was rapidly getting the better of him. 'I can't think what your father was thinking of to let a pret—to let a girl like you come away like this.'

'If you were going to say pretty girl,' said Miss Cringle, with calm self-abnegation, 'don't mind me, say it. The captain knows what he's about. He told me you were a milksop; he said you were a good young man and a teetotaller.'

The mate, allowing the truth of the captain's statement as to his abstinence, hotly denied the charge of goodness. 'I can understand your father's hurry to get rid of you for a spell,' he concluded, being goaded beyond all considerations of politeness. 'His gout would never get well while you were with him. More than that, I shouldn't wonder if you were the cause of it.'

With this parting shot he departed, before the girl could think of a suitable reply, and went and sulked in the dingy little fo'c'sle.

In the evening, the weather having moderated somewhat, and the tide being on the ebb, they got under way again, the girl coming on deck fully attired in an oilskin coat and sou'-wester to resume the command. The rain fell steadily as they ploughed along their way, guided by the bright eye of the 'Mouse' as it shone across the darkening waters. The mate, soaked to the skin, was at the wheel.

'Why don't you go below and put your oilskins on?' inquired the girl, when this fact dawned upon her.

'Don't want them,' said the mate.

'I suppose you know best,' said the girl, and said no more

until nine o'clock, when she paused at the companion to give her last orders for the night.

'I'm going to turn in,' said she; 'call me at two o'clock. Good night.'

'Good night,' said the other, and the girl vanished.

Left to himself, the mate, who began to feel chilly, felt in his pockets for a pipe, and was in all the stress of getting a light, when he heard a thin, almost mild voice behind him, and, looking round, saw the face of the girl at the companion.

'I say, are these your oilskins I've been wearing?' she demanded awkwardly.

'You're quite welcome,' said the mate.

'Why didn't you tell me?' said the girl indignantly. 'I wouldn't have worn them for anything if I had known it.'

'Well, they won't poison you,' said the mate resentfully. 'Your father left his at Ipswich to have them cobbled up a bit.'

The girl passed them up on the deck, and, closing the companion with a bang, disappeared. It is possible that the fatigues of the day had been too much for her, for when she awoke, and consulted the little silver watch that hung by her bunk, it was past five o'clock, and the red glow of the sun was flooding the cabin as she arose and hastily dressed.

The deck was drying in white patches as she went above, and the mate was sitting yawning at the wheel, his eyelids red for want of sleep.

'Didn't I tell you to call me at two o'clock?' she demanded confronting him.

'It's all right,' said the mate. 'I thought when you woke would be soon enough. You looked tired.'

'I think you'd better go when we get to Ipswich,' said the girl, tightening her lips. 'I'll ship somebody who'll obey orders.'

'I'll go when we get back to London,' said the mate. 'I'll hand this barge over to the cap'n and nobody else.'

51

'Well, we'll see,' said the girl, as she took the wheel. '*I* think you'll go at Ipswich.'

For the remainder of the voyage the subject was not alluded to; the mate, in a spirit of sulky pride, kept to the fore part of the boat, except when he was steering, and, as far as practicable, the girl ignored his presence. In this spirit of mutual forbearance they entered the Orwell, and ran swiftly up to Ipswich.

It was late in the afternoon when they arrived there, and the new skipper, waiting only until they were made fast, went ashore, leaving the mate in charge. She had been gone about an hour when a small telegraph boy appeared, and, after boarding the barge in the unsafest manner possible, handed him a telegram. The mate read it and his face flushed. With even more than the curtness customary in language at a halfpenny a word, it contained his dismissal.

'I've had a telegram from your father sacking me,' he said to the girl, as she returned soon after, laden with small parcels.

'Yes, I wired him to,' she replied calmly. 'I suppose you'll go *now*?'

'I'd rather go back to London with you,' he said slowly.

'I daresay,' said the girl. 'As a matter of fact I wasn't really meaning you to go, but when you said you wouldn't I thought we'd see who was master. I've shipped another mate, so you see I haven't lost much time.'

'Who is he,' inquired the mate.

'Man named Charlie Lee,' replied the girl; 'the foreman here told me of him.'

'He'd no business to,' said the mate, frowning; 'he's a loose fish; take my advice and ship somebody else. He's not at all the sort of chap I'd choose for you to sail with.'

'You'd choose,' said the girl scornfully; 'dear me, what a pity you didn't tell me before.'

'He's a loafer,' said the mate, meeting her eye angrily, 'and about as bad they make them; but I suppose you'll have your own way.'

'He won't frighten me,' said the girl. 'I'm quite capable of taking care of myself, thank you. Good evening.'

The mate stepped ashore with a small bundle, leaving the remainder of his possessions to go back to London with the barge. The girl watched his well-knit figure as it strode up the quay until it was out of sight, and then, inwardly piqued because he had not turned round for a parting glance, gave a little sigh, and went below to tea.

The docile and respectful behaviour of the newcomer was a pleasant change to the autocrat of the *Osprey*, and cargoes were worked out and in without an unpleasant word. They laid at the quay for two days, the new mate, whose home was at Ipswich, sleeping ashore, and on the morning of the third he turned up punctually at six o'clock, and they started on their return voyage.

'Well, you do know to handle a craft,' said Lee admiringly, as they passed down the river. 'The old boat seems to know it's got a pretty young lady in charge.'

'Don't talk rubbish,' said the girl austerely.

The new mate carefully adjusted his red necktie and smiled indulgently.

'Well, you're the prettiest cap'n I've ever sailed under,' he said. 'What do they call that red cap you've got on? Tam-o'-Shanter is it?'

'I don't know,' said the girl shortly.

'You mean you won't tell me,' said the other, with a look of anger in his soft dark eyes.

'Just as you like,' said she, and Lee, whistling softly, turned on his heel and began to busy himself with some small matter forward.

The rest of the day passed quietly, though there was a freedom in the new mate's manner which made the redoubtable skipper of the *Osprey* regret her change of crew, and to treat him with more civility than her proud spirit quite approved of. There was but little wind, and the barge merely crawled along as the captain and mate, with surreptitious glances, took each other's measure.

'This is the nicest trip I've ever had,' said Lee, as he came up from an unduly prolonged tea, with a strong-smelling cigar in his mouth. 'I've brought your jacket up.'

'I don't want it, thank you,' said the girl.

'Better have it,' said Lee, holding it up for her.

'When I want my jacket I'll put it on myself,' said the girl.

'All right, no offence,' said the other airily. 'What an obstinate creature you are.'

'Have you got any drink down there?' inquired the girl, eyeing him sternly.

'Just a little drop of whisky, my dear, for the spasms,' said Lee facetiously. 'Will you have some?'

'I won't have any drinking here,' said she sharply. 'If you want to drink, wait till you get ashore.'

'*You* won't have any drinking!' said the other, opening his eyes, and with a quiet chuckle he dived below and brought up a bottle and a glass. 'Here's wishing a better temper to you, my dear,' he said amiably. 'Come you'd better have some. It'll put a little colour in your cheeks.'

'Put it away now, there's a good fellow,' said the captain timidly, as she looked anxiously at the nearest sail, some two miles distant.

'It's the only friend I've got,' said Lee, sprawling gracefully on the hatches, and replenishing his glass. 'Look here. Are you on for a bargain?'

'What do you mean?' inquired the girl.

'Give me a kiss and I won't take another drink tonight,' said the new mate tenderly. 'Come, I won't tell.'

'I'll never do that,' said the girl, striving to speak calmly. 'Don't talk nonsense to me again.'

Now thoroughly frightened, the girl at the wheel steered in silence.

'Better get the side-lights out,' she said at length.

'Plenty of time,' said Lee.

'Take the helm, then, while I do it,' said the girl, biting her lips.

The fellow rose and came towards her, and, as she made way for him, threw his arm round her waist and tried to detain her. Her heart beating quickly, she walked forward, and, not without a hesitating glance at the figure at the wheel, descended into the fo'c'sle for the lamps.

The next moment, with a gasping cry, she sank down on a locker as the dark figure of a man rose and stood by her.

'Don't be frightened,' it said quietly.

'Jack?' said the girl.

'That's me,' said the figure. 'You didn't expect to see me, did you? I thought perhaps you didn't know what was good for you, so I stowed myself away last night, and here I am.'

'Have you heard what that fellow has been saying to me?' demanded Miss Cringle, with a spice of the old temper leavening her voice once more.

'Every word,' said the mate cheerfully.

'Why didn't you come up and stand by me?' inquired the girl hotly.

The mate hung his head.

'Oh,' said the girl, and her tones were those of acute disappointment, 'you're afraid.'

'I'm not,' said the mate scornfully.

'Why didn't you come up, then, instead of skulking down here?' inquired the girl.

The mate scratched the back of his neck and smiled, but weakly. 'Well, I—I thought——' he began, and stopped.

'You thought——' prompted Miss Cringle coldly.

'I thought a little fright would do you good,' said the mate speaking quickly, 'and that it would make you appreciate me a little more when I did come.'

'Ahoy! *Maggie! Maggie!*' came the voice of the graceless varlet who was steering.

'I'll *Maggie* him,' said the mate, grinding his teeth. 'Why, what—why you're crying.'

'I'm not,' sobbed Miss Cringle scornfully, 'I'm in a temper that's all.'

'I'll knock his head off,' said the mate; 'you stay down here.'

'Mag-*gie!*' came the voice again, '*Mag*—HULLO!'

'Where you calling me, my lad?' said the mate, with dangerous politeness, as he stepped aft. 'Aren't you afraid of straining that sweet voice of yours? Let go of that tiller.'

The other let go, and the mate's fist took him heavily in the face and sent him sprawling on the deck. He rose with a scream of rage and rushed at his opponent, but the mate's temper, which had suffered badly through his treatment of the last few days, was up, and he sent him heavily down again.

'There's a little dark dingy hole forward,' said the mate, after waiting some time for him to rise again, 'just the place for you to go and think over your sins. If I see you come out of it until we get to London, I'll hurt you. Now clear.'

The other cleared, and, carefully avoiding the girl, who was standing close by, disappeared below.

'You've hurt him,' said the girl, coming up to the mate and laying her hand on his arm. 'What a horrid temper you've got.'

'It was him asking you to kiss him that upset me,' said the mate apologetically.

'He put his arm round my waist,' said Miss Cringle, blushing.

'*What!*' said the mate, stuttering, 'put his—put his arm—round—your waist—like——'

56

His courage suddenly forsook him.

'Like what?' inquired the girl, with superb innocence.

'Like *that*,' said the mate manfully.

'That'll do,' said Miss Cringle softly, 'that'll do. You're as bad as he is, only the worst of it is there is nobody here to prevent you.'

In Borrowed Plumes

THE master of the *Sarah Jane* had been missing for two days, and all on board, with the exception of the boy, whom nobody troubled about, were full of joy at the circumstance. Twice before the skipper, whose habits might, perhaps, be best described as irregular, missed his ship, and word had gone forth that the third time would be the last. His berth was a good one, and the mate wanted it in place of his own, which in turn was wanted by Ted Jones, A.B.

'Two hours more,' said the mate anxiously to the men, as they stood leaning against the side, 'and I take the ship out.'

'Under two hours'll do it,' said Ted, peering over the side and watching the water as it slowly rose over the mud. 'What's got the old man, I wonder?'

'I don't know, and I don't care,' said the mate. 'You chaps stand by me and it'll be good for all of us. Mr Pearson said distinctly the last time, that if the skipper ever missed his ship again it would be his last trip in her, and he told me before the old man that I wasn't to wait two minutes at any time, but to bring her out right away.'

'He's an old fool,' said Bill Loch, the other hand; 'and nobody'll miss him but the boy, and he's been looking regular worried all the morning. Look at him now.'

The mate gave a supercilious glance in the direction of the

boy, and then turned away. The boy, who had no idea of courting observation, stowed himself away behind the windlass; and, taking a letter from his pocket, perused it for the fourth time.

'Dear Tommy,' it began. 'I take my pen in hand to inform you that I'm staying here and can't get away for the reason that I lost my clothes at cribbage last night. Also my money and everything else as well. Don't speak to a living soul about it as the mate wants my berth, but pack up some clothes and bring them to me without saying anything to anybody. The mate's clothes will do because I haven't got another suit, but don't tell him. You needn't trouble about socks as I've got them left. My head is so bad I must now conclude. Your affectionate uncle and captain, Joe Bross. P.S. Don't let the mate see you come, or he won't let you go.'

'Two hours more,' sighed Tommy, as he put the letter back in his pocket. 'How can I get any clothes when they're all locked up? And Aunt said I was to look after him and see he didn't get into mischief.'

He sat thinking deeply, and then, as the crew of the *Sarah Jane* stepped ashore to take advantage of a glass offered by the mate, he crept down to the cabin again for another desperate look round. The only articles of clothing visible belonged to Mrs Bross, who up to this trip had been sailing in the schooner to look after its master. At these he gazed hard.

'I'll take them and try to change them for some men's clothes,' said he suddenly, snatching the garments from the pegs. 'She wouldn't mind'; and hastily rolling them into a parcel, together with a pair of carpet slippers of the captain's, he thrust the lot into an old biscuit bag. Then he shouldered his burden, and, going cautiously on deck, gained the shore, and set off at a trot to the address furnished in the letter.

It was a long way, and the bag was heavy. His first attempt at barter was alarming, for the pawnbroker, who had just been cautioned by the police, was in such a severe and uncomfortable state of morals, that the boy quickly snatched up his bundle again and left. Sorely troubled he walked hastily along, until, in a small side street, his glance fell upon a baker of mild and benevolent aspect, standing behind the counter of his shop.

'If you please, sir,' said Tommy, entering, and depositing his bag on the counter, 'have you got any cast-off clothes you don't want?'

The baker turned to a shelf, and selecting a stale loaf cut it in halves, one of which he placed before the boy.

'I don't want bread,' said Tommy desperately; 'but Mother has just died, and Father wants mourning for the funeral. He's only got a new suit with him, and if he can change these things of Mother's for an old suit, he'd sell his best one for money to bury her with.'

He shook the articles out on the counter, and the baker's wife, who had just come into the shop, inspected them rather favourably.

'Poor boy, so you've lost your mother,' she said, turning the clothes over. 'It's a good skirt, Bill.'

'Yes, ma'am,' said Tommy dolefully.

'What did she die of?' inquired the baker.

'Scarlet fever,' said Tommy, tearfully, mentioning the only disease he knew.

'Scar—— Take those things away,' yelled the baker, pushing the clothes on to the floor, and following his wife to the other end of the shop. 'Take them away at once, you young villain.'

His voice was so loud, his manner so imperative, that the startled boy, without stopping to argue, stuffed the clothes pell-mell into the bag again and departed. A farewell glance at the clock made him look almost as horrified as the baker.

'There's no time to be lost,' he muttered, as he began to run;

'either the old man'll have to come in these or else stay where he is.'

He reached the house breathless, and paused before an unshaven man in worn greasy clothes, who was smoking a short clay pipe with much enjoyment in front of the door.

'Is Cap'n Bross here?' he panted.

'He's upstairs,' said the man, with a leer, 'sitting in sack-cloth and ashes. Have you got some clothes for him?'

'Look here,' said Tommy. He was down on his knees with the mouth of the bag open again, quite in the style of a practised hawker. 'Give me an old suit of clothes for them. Hurry up. There's a lovely frock.'

'Blimey,' said the man, staring. 'I've only got these clothes. What d'you take me for. A duke?'

'Well, get me some somewhere,' said Tommy. 'If you don't the cap'n'll have to come in these, and I'm sure he won't like it.'

'I wonder what he'd look like,' said the man, with a grin. 'Dashed if I don't come up and see.'

'Get me some clothes,' pleaded Tommy.

'I wouldn't get you clothes, not for fifty pounds,' said the man severely. 'What d'you mean spoiling other people's pleasure that way? Come on, come and tell the cap'n what you've got for him, I want to hear what he says. He's been swearing hard since ten o'clock this morning, but he ought to say something special about this.'

He led the way up the bare wooden stairs, followed by the harassed boy, and entered a small dirty room at the top, in the centre of which the master of the *Sarah Jane* sat.

'Here's a young man come to bring you some clothes, cap'n,' said the man, taking the sack from the boy.

'Why didn't you come before?' growled the captain.

The man put his hand in the sack, and pulled out the clothes. 'What do you think of them?' he asked expectantly.

The captain strove vainly to tell him, but his tongue

mercifully forsook its office, and dried between his lips. His brain rang with sentences of scorching iniquity, but they got no further.

'Well, say thank you, if you can't say anything else,' suggested his tormentor hopefully.

'I couldn't bring anything else,' said Tommy hurriedly; 'everything was locked up. I tried to get them changed and nearly got locked up myself. Put these on and hurry up.'

The captain moistened his lips with his tongue.

'The mate'll get off directly she floats,' continued Tommy. 'Put these on and spoil his little game. It's raining a little now. Nobody'll see you, and as soon as you get aboard you can borrow some of the men's clothes.'

'That's the ticket, cap'n,' said the man. 'Good gracious, you'll have everybody falling in love with you.'

'Hurry up,' said Tommy, dancing with impatience. 'Hurry up.'

The skipper, dazed and wild-eyed, stood still while his two assistants hastily dressed him. Tommy stood up on tip-toe to tie the skipper's bonnet on. 'Now tie the scarf over his chin to hide his beard, and put this veil on. It's a good job he hasn't got a moustache.'

The other complied, and then fell back a pace or two to gaze at his handiwork. 'Well, though I say it myself, you look a treat!' he remarked complacently. 'Now, young man, take hold of his arm. Go up the back streets, and if you see anybody looking at you, call him Ma'am.'

The two set off and fortunately for the success of the venture, it was pelting with rain. Though a few people gazed curiously at the couple as they went hastily along, they were unmolested, and gained the wharf in safety, arriving just in time to see the schooner shoving off from the side.

At the sight the skipper held up his skirts and ran. 'Ahoy!' he shouted. 'Wait a minute.'

The mate gave one look of blank astonishment at the

extraordinary figure, and then turned away; but at that moment the stern came within jumping distance of the wharf, and uncle and nephew moved with one impulse, leaped for it, and gained the deck in safety.

'Why didn't you wait when I hailed you?' demanded the skipper fiercely.

'How was I to know it was you?' inquired the mate surlily, as he realized his defeat. 'I thought it was the Empress of Russia.'

The skipper stared at him dumbly.

'And if you take my advice,' said the mate, with a sneer, 'you'll keep those things on. *I've* never seen you look so well in anything before.'

'I want to borrow some of your clothes, Bob,' said the skipper, eyeing him steadily.

'Where's your own?' asked the other.

'I don't know,' said the skipper. 'I was taken with a fit last night, Bob, and when I woke up this morning they were gone. Somebody must have taken advantage of my helpless state and taken them.'

'Very likely,' said the mate, turning away to shout an order to the crew, who were busy setting sail.

'Where are they, old man?' inquired the skipper.

'How should I know?' asked the other, becoming interested in the men again.

'I mean *your* clothes,' said the skipper, who was fast losing his temper.

'Oh, mine?' said the mate. 'Well, as a matter of fact, I don't like lending my clothes. I'm rather particular. You might have a fit in *them*.'

'You won't lend them to me?' asked the skipper.

'I won't,' said the mate, speaking loudly, and frowning significantly at the crew, who were listening.

'Very good,' said the skipper. 'Ted, come here. Where's your other clothes?'

'I'm very sorry, sir,' said Ted shifting uneasily from one leg to the other, and glancing at the mate for support; 'but they aren't fit for you to wear, sir.'

'I'm the best judge of that,' said the skipper sharply. 'Bring them here.'

'Well, to tell the truth, sir,' said Ted, 'I'm like the mate. I'm only a poor sailor, but I wouldn't lend my clothes to the Queen of England.'

'You fetch those clothes,' roared the skipper snatching off his bonnet and flinging it on the deck. 'Fetch them at once. D'you think I'm going about in these petticoats?'

'They're my clothes,' muttered Ted doggedly.

'Very well, then, I'll have Bill's,' said the skipper. 'But mind you, my lad, I'll make you pay for this before I've done with you. Bill's the only honest man aboard this ship. Give me your hand, Bill, old man.'

'I'm with those two,' said Bill gruffly, as he turned away.

The skipper, biting his lips with fury, turned from one to the other, and then, with a big oath, walked forward. Before he could reach the fo'c'sle Bill and Ted dived down before him, and, by the time he had descended, sat on their sea-chests side by side confronting him. To threats and appeals alike they turned a deaf ear, and the frantic skipper was compelled at last to go on deck again, still encumbered with the hated skirts.

'Why don't you go and lie down,' said the mate, 'and I'll send you down a nice cup of hot tea. You'll get hysterics if you go on like that.'

'I'll knock your head off if you talk to me,' said the skipper.

'Not you,' said the mate cheerfully; 'you aren't big enough. Look at that poor fellow over there.'

The skipper looked in the direction indicated, and, swelling with impotent rage, shook his fist fiercely at a red-faced man with grey whiskers, who was wafting innumerable tender kisses from the bridge of a passing steamer.

'That's right,' said the mate approvingly; 'don't give him any encouragement. Love at first sight isn't worth having.'

The skipper, suffering severely from suppressed emotion, went below, and the crew, after waiting a little while to make sure that he was not coming up again, made their way quietly to the mate.

'If we can only take him to Battlesea in this rig it'll be all right,' said the latter. 'You chaps stand by me. His slippers and sou'wester are the only clothes he's got aboard. Throw every needle you can lay your hands on overboard, or else he'll be trying to make a suit out of a piece of old sail or something. If we can only take him to Mr Pearson like this, it won't be so bad after all.'

While these arrangements were in hand above, the skipper and the boy were busy over others below. Various startling schemes propounded by the skipper for obtaining possession of his men's attire were rejected by the youth as unlawful, and, what was worse, impracticable. For a couple of hours they discussed ways and means, but only ended in diatribes against the mean ways of the crew; and the skipper fell into a state of sullen despair at length, and sat silent.

'By George, Tommy, I've got it,' he cried suddenly, starting up and hitting the table with his fist. 'Where's your other suit?'

'That isn't any bigger than this one,' said Tommy.

'You get it out,' said the skipper, with a knowing toss of his head. 'Ah, there we are. Now go in my state-room and take those off.'

The wondering Tommy, who thought that great grief had turned his kinsman's brain, complied, and emerged shortly afterwards in a blanket, bringing his clothes under his arm.

'Now, do you know what I'm going to do?' inquired the skipper, with a big smile.

'No.'

'Fetch me the scissors. Now do you know what I'm going to do then?'

'Cut up the two suits and make them into one,' hazarded the horror-stricken Tommy. 'Here, stop it! Leave off!'

The skipper pushed him impatiently off, and, placing the clothes on the table, took up the scissors, and, with a few slashing strokes, cut those garments into their component parts.

'What am *I* to wear,' said Tommy, beginning to sob. 'You didn't think of that?'

'What are you to wear, you selfish young puppy?' said the skipper sternly. 'Always thinking about yourself. Go and get some needles and thread, and if there's anything left over, and you're a good boy, I'll see whether I can't make something for you out of it.'

'There aren't any needles here,' whined Tommy, after a lengthened search.

'Go down to the fo'c'sle and get the case of sail-makers' needles, then,' said the skipper. 'Don't let anyone see what you're after, and bring some thread.'

'Well, why couldn't you let me go in my clothes before you cut them up,' moaned Tommy. 'I don't like going up in this blanket. They'll laugh at me.'

'You go at once!' thundered the skipper, and, turning his back on him, whistled softly, and began to arrange the pieces of cloth.

'Laugh away, my lads,' he said cheerfully, as an uproarious burst of laughter greeted the appearance of Tommy on deck. 'Wait a bit.'

He waited himself for nearly twenty minutes, at the end of which time Tommy, treading on his blanket, came flying down the companion-ladder, and rolled into the cabin.

'There isn't a needle aboard the ship,' he said solemnly, as he picked himself up and rubbed his head. 'I've looked everywhere.'

'What?' roared the skipper, hastily concealing the pieces of cloth. 'Here, Ted! Ted!'

'Ay, ay, sir!' said Ted, as he came below.

'I want a sail-maker's needle,' said the skipper glibly. 'I've got a rent in this skirt.'

'I broke the last one yesterday,' said Ted, with an evil grin.

'Any other needle then,' said the skipper, trying to conceal his emotion.

'I don't believe there's such a thing aboard the ship,' said Ted, who had obeyed the mate's thoughtful injunction. '*Nor* thread. I was only saying so to the mate yesterday.'

The skipper sank again to the lowest depths, waved him away, and then, getting on a corner of the locker, fell into a gloomy reverie.

'It's a pity you do things in such a hurry,' said Tommy, sniffing vindictively. 'You might have made sure of the needle before you spoiled my clothes. There's two of us going about in a ridiculous fashion now.'

The master of the *Sarah Jane* allowed this insolence to pass unheeded.

Once out of the river he came on deck again, and, ignoring by a great effort the smiles of the crew and the jibes of the mate, took command. The only alteration he made in his dress was to substitute his sou'wester for the bonnet, and in this guise he did his work while the aggrieved Tommy hopped about in blankets. The three days at sea passed like a horrid dream. So covetous was his gaze, that the crew instinctively clutched their nether garments and looked to the buttoning of their coats as they passed him. He saw coats in the mainsail, and fashioned phantom trousers out of the flying jib, and towards the end began to babble of blue serges and mixed tweeds. Oblivious of fame, he had resolved to enter the harbour of Battlesea by night; but it was not to be. Near home the wind dropped, and the sun was well up before Battlesea came into view, a grey bank on the starboard bow.

Until within a mile of the harbour, the skipper held on, and then his grasp of the wheel relaxed somewhat, and he looked round anxiously for the mate.

'Where's Bob?' he shouted.

'He's very ill, sir,' said Ted, shaking his head.

'Ill?' gasped the startled skipper. 'Here, take the wheel a minute.'

He handed it over, and grasping his skirts went hastily below. The mate was half lying, half sitting, in his bunk, groaning dismally.

'What's the matter?' inquired the skipper.

'I'm dying,' said the mate. 'I keep being tied up all in knots inside. I can't hold myself straight.'

The other cleared his throat. 'You'd better take off your clothes and lie down a bit,' he said kindly. 'Let me help you off with them.'

'No—don't—trouble,' panted the mate.

'It isn't any trouble,' said the skipper, in a trembling voice.

'No, I'll keep them on,' said the mate faintly. 'I've always had an idea I'd like to die in my clothes. It may be foolish, but I can't help it.'

'You'll have your wish some day, never fear, you infernal rascal,' shouted the overwrought skipper. 'You're shamming sickness to make me take the ship into port.'

'Why shouldn't you take her in,' asked the mate, with an air of innocent surprise. 'It's your duty as cap'n. You'd better get above now. The bar is always shifting.'

The skipper, restraining himself by a mighty effort, went on deck again, and, taking the wheel, addressed the crew. He

68

spoke feelingly of the obedience men owed their superior officers, and the moral obligation they were under to lend them their trousers when they required them. He dwelt on the awful punishments awarded for mutiny, and proved clearly, that to allow the master of a ship to enter port in petticoats was mutiny of the worst type. He then sent them below for their clothing. They were gone such a long time that it was palpable to the meanest intellect that they did not intend to bring it. Meanwhile the harbour widened out before him.

There were two or three people on the quay as the *Sarah Jane* came within hailing distance. By the time she had passed the lantern at the end of it there were two or three dozen, and the numbers were steadily increasing at the rate of three persons for every five yards she made. Kind-hearted, humane men, anxious that their friends should not lose so great and cheap a treat, bribed small and reluctant boys with pennies to go in search of them, and by the time the schooner reached her berth, a large proportion of the population of the port was looking over each other's shoulders and shouting foolish and hilarious inquiries to the skipper. The news reached the owner, and he came hurrying down to the ship, just as the skipper, regardless of the heated remonstrances of the sight-seers, was preparing to go below.

Mr Pearson was a stout man, and he came down exploding with wrath. Then he saw the apparition, and mirth overcame him. It became necessary for three stout fellows to act as buttresses, and the more indignant the skipper looked, the harder their work became. Finally he was assisted, in a weak state, and laughing hysterically, to the deck of the schooner, where he followed the skipper below, and in a voice broken with emotion demanded an explanation.

'It's the finest sight I ever saw in my life, Bross,' he said when the other had finished. 'I wouldn't have missed it for anything. I've been feeling very low this last week, and it's done me good. Don't talk nonsense about leaving the ship. I wouldn't lose you for anything after this, but if you like to ship a fresh mate and crew you can please yourself. If you'll only come up to the house and let Mrs Pearson see you—she's been ailing—I'll give you a couple of pounds. Now, get your bonnet and come.'

The Boatswain's Watch

CAPTAIN POLSON sat in his comfortable parlour smiling benignly upon his daughter and sister. His ship, after an absence of eighteen months, was once more berthed in the small harbour of Barborough, and the captain was sitting in that state of good-natured affability which invariably characterized his first appearance after a long absence.

'No news this end, I suppose,' he inquired, after a lengthy recital of most extraordinarily uninteresting adventures.

'Not much,' said his sister Jane, looking nervously at her niece. 'Young Metcalfe has gone into partnership with his father.'

'I don't want to hear about those sharks,' said the captain, waxing red. 'Tell me about honest men.'

'Joe Lewis has had a month's imprisonment for stealing fowls,' said Miss Polson meekly. 'Mrs Purton has had twins—dear little fellows they are, fat as butter!—she has named one of them Polson, after you. The greedy one.'

'Any deaths?' inquired the captain snappishly, as he eyed the innocent lady suspiciously.

'Poor old Jasper Wheeler has gone,' said his sister; 'he was very resigned. He borrowed enough money to get a big doctor from London, and when he heard that there was no hope for him he said he was just longing to go, and he was sorry he couldn't take all his dear ones with him. Mary Hewson is married to Jack Draper, and young Metcalfe's banns go up for the third time next Sunday.'

'I hope he gets a Tartar,' said the vindictive captain. 'Who's the girl? Some silly little fool, I know. She ought to be warned!'

'I don't believe in interfering in marriages,' said his daughter Chrissie, shaking her head sagely.

'Oh!' said the captain, staring, '*you* don't! Now you've your hair up and taken to wearing long frocks, I suppose you're beginning to think of it.'

'Yes; Auntie wants to tell you something!' said his daughter, rising and crossing the room.

'No, I don't!' said Miss Polson hastily.

'You'd better do it,' said Chrissie, giving her a little push, 'there's a dear; I'll go upstairs and lock myself in my room.'

The face of the captain, whilst this conversation was passing, was a study in suppressed emotions. He was a firm advocate of importing the manners of the quarter-deck into private life, the only drawback being that he had to leave behind him the language usual in that locality. To this omission he usually ascribed his failures.

'Sit down, Chrissie,' he commanded; 'sit down, Jane. Now, miss, what's all this about?'

'I don't like to tell you,' said Chrissie, folding her hands in her lap. 'I know you'll be cross. You're so unreasonable.'

The captain stared—frightfully.

'I'm going to be married,' said Chrissie suddenly—'there! To Jack Metcalfe—there! So you'll have to learn to love him. He's going to try and love you for my sake.' To his sister's dismay the captain got up, and brandishing his fists walked violently to and fro. By these simple but unusual means decorum was preserved.

'If you were only a boy,' said the captain, when he had regained his seat, 'I should know what to do with you.'

'If I were a boy,' said Chrissie, who, having braced herself up for the fray, meant to go through with it, 'I shouldn't want to marry Jack. Don't be silly, Father!'

'Jane,' said the captain, in a voice which made the lady addressed start in her chair, 'what do you mean by it?'

'It wasn't my fault,' said Miss Polson feebly. 'I told her how it would be. And it was so gradual; he admired my geraniums at first, and, of course, I was deceived. There are so many people admire my geraniums; whether it is because the window has a south aspect——'

'Oh!' said the captain rudely, 'that'll do, Jane. If he wasn't a lawyer, I'd go round and break his neck. Chrissie is only nineteen, and she'll come for a year's cruise with me. Perhaps the sea air'll strengthen her head. We'll see who's master in this family.'

'I'm sure I don't want to be master,' said his daughter, taking a weapon of fine cambric out of her pocket, and getting ready for action. 'I can't help liking people. Auntie likes him too, don't you Auntie?'

'Yes,' said Miss Polson bravely.

'Very good,' said the autocrat promptly, 'I'll take you both for a cruise.'

'You're making me very un—unhappy,' said Chrissie, burying her face in her handkerchief.

'You'll be more unhappy before I've done with you,' said the captain grimly. 'And while I think of it, I'll step round and stop those banns.'

His daughter caught him by the arm as he was passing, and laid her face on his sleeve. 'You'll make me look so foolish,' she wailed.

'That'll make it easier for you to come to sea with me,' said her father. 'Don't cry all over my sleeve. I'm going to see a parson. Run upstairs and play with your dolls, and if you're a good girl, I'll bring you in some sweets.' He put on his hat, and closing the front door with a bang, went off to the new rector to knock two years off the age which his daughter kept for purposes of matrimony. The rector, grieved at such duplicity in one so young, met him more than half-way, and he came out from him smiling placidly, until his attention was attracted by a young man on the other side of the road, who was regarding him with manifest awkwardness.

'Good evening, Captain Polson,' he said, crossing the road.

'Oh,' said the captain, stopping, 'I wanted to speak to you. I suppose you wanted to marry my daughter while I was out of the way, to save trouble. Just the manly thing I should have expected of you. I've stopped the banns, and I'm going to take her for a voyage with me. You'll have to look elsewhere my lad.'

'The ill feeling is all on your side, captain,' said Metcalfe, reddening.

'Ill feeling!' snorted the captain. 'You put me in the witness-box, and made me a laughing-stock in the place with your silly attempts at jokes, lost me five hundred pounds, and then try and marry my daughter while I'm at sea. Ill feeling be hanged!'

'That was business,' said the other.

'It was,' said the captain, 'and this is business too. Mine. I'll look after it, I'll promise you. I think I know who'll look silly this time. I'd sooner see my girl in heaven than married to a rascal of a lawyer.'

'You'd want good glasses,' retorted Metcalfe, who was becoming ruffled.

'I don't want to bandy words with you,' said the captain with dignity, after a long pause, devoted to thinking of something worth bandying. 'You think you're a clever fellow, but I know a cleverer. You're quite welcome to marry my daughter —if you can.'

He turned on his heel, and refusing to listen to any further remarks, went on his way rejoicing. Arrived home, he lit his pipe, and throwing himself into an armchair, related his

74

exploits. Chrissie had recourse to her handkerchief again, more for effect than use, but Miss Polson, who was a tender soul, took hers out and wept unrestrainedly. At first the captain took it well enough. It was a tribute to his power, but when they took to sobbing one against the other, his temper rose, and he sternly commanded silence.

'I shall be like—this—every day at sea,' sobbed Chrissie vindictively, 'only worse; making us all ridiculous.'

'Stop that noise at once!' vociferated the captain.

'We c-c-can't,' sobbed Miss Polson.

'And we d-don't want to,' said Chrissie. 'It's all we can do, and we're going to do it. You'd better g-go out and stop something else. You can't stop us.'

The captain took the advice and went, and in the billiard-room of the George heard some news which set him thinking, and which brought him back somewhat earlier than he had at first intended. A small group at his gate broke up into its elements at his approach, and the captain, following his sister and daughter into the room, sat down and eyed them severely.

'So you're going to run off to London to get married, are you, miss?' he said ferociously. 'Well, we'll see. You don't go out of my sight until we sail, and if I catch that pettifogging lawyer round at my gate again, I'll break every bone in his body, mind that.'

For the next three days the captain kept his daughter under observation, and never allowed her to stir abroad except in his company. The evening of the third day, to his own great surprise, he spent at a gathering of charitably-minded ladies who were working to provide garments for the poor. The company was not congenial, several of the ladies putting their work away, and glaring frigidly at the intruder; and though they could see clearly that he was suffering greatly, made no attempt to put him at his ease. He was very thoughtful all the way home, and the next day took a partner into the concern, in the shape of his boatswain.

'You understand, Tucker,' he concluded, as the hapless man stood in a cringing attitude before Chrissie, 'that you never let my daughter out of your sight. When she goes out you go with her.'

'Yessir,' said Tucker; 'and suppose she tells me to go home, what am I to do then?'

'You're a fool,' said the captain sharply. 'It doesn't matter what she says or does; unless you are in the same room, you are never to be more than three yards from her.'

'Make it four, cap'n,' said the boatswain, in a broken voice.

'Three,' said the captain; 'and mind, she's artful. All girls are, and she'll try and give you the slip. I've had information given me as to what's going on. Whatever happens, you are not to leave her.'

'I wish you'd get somebody else, sir,' said Tucker, very respectfully. 'There's a lot of chaps aboard who'd like the job.'

'You're the only man I can trust,' said the captain shortly. 'When I give you orders I know they'll be obeyed; it's your watch now.'

He went out humming. Chrissie took up a book and sat down, utterly ignoring the woebegone figure which stood the regulation three yards from her, twisting its cap in its hands.

'I hope, miss,' said the boatswain, after standing patiently for three-quarters of an hour, 'that you don't think I sought after this little job.'

'No,' said Chrissie, without looking up.

'I'm just obeying orders,' continued the boatswain. 'I always get let in for these little jobs somehow. The monkeys I've had to look after aboard ship would frighten you. There never was a monkey on the *Monarch* that I wasn't put in charge. That's what a man gets through being trustworthy.'

'Just so,' said Chrissie, putting down her book. 'Well, I'm going into the kitchen now; come along, nursie.'

'Here, I say, miss!' remonstrated Tucker, flushing.

'I don't know how Susan will like you going into her kitchen,' said Chrissie thoughtfully; 'however, that's your business.'

The unfortunate seaman followed his fair charge into the kitchen, and, leaning against the doorpost, doubled up like a limp rag before the terrible glance of its mistress.

'Ho!' said Susan, who took the state of affairs as an insult to the sex in general; 'and what might you be wanting?'

'Cap'n's orders,' murmured Tucker feebly.

'I'm captain here,' said Susan, confronting him with her bare arms akimbo.

'And credit it does you,' said the boatswain looking round admiringly.

'Is it your wish Miss Chrissie, that this image comes stalking into my kitchen as if the place belongs to him?' demanded the irate Susan.

'I didn't mean to come in that way,' said the astonished Tucker. 'I can't help being big.'

'I don't want him here,' said her mistress; 'what do you think I want him for?'

'You hear that?' said Susan, pointing to the door; 'now go. I don't want people to say that you come into this kitchen after me.'

'I'm here by the cap'n's orders,' said Tucker faintly. 'I don't want to be here—far from it. As for people saying that I come here after you, anyone who knows me would laugh at the idea.'

'If I had my way,' said Susan, in a hard rasping voice, 'I'd box your ears for you, and you can go and tell the cap'n I said so. Spy!'

This was the first verse of the first watch, and there were many verses. To add to his discomfort he was confined to the house, as his charge manifested no desire to go outside, and as neither she nor her aunt cared about the trouble of bringing him to a fit and proper state of subjection, the task became a labour of love for the energetic Susan. In spite of everything, however, he stuck to his guns, and the indignant Chrissie, who was in almost hourly communication with Metcalfe through the medium of her faithful handmaiden, was rapidly becoming desperate.

On the fourth day, time getting short, Chrissie went on a new tack with her keeper, and Susan, sorely against her will, had to follow suit. Chrissie smiled at him, Susan called him Mr Tucker, and Miss Polson gave him a glass of her best wine. From the position of an outcast, he jumped in one bound to that of confidential adviser. Miss Polson told him many items of family interest, and later on in the afternoon actually consulted him with regard to a bad cold Chrissie had developed.

He prescribed half a pint of linseed oil hot, but Miss Polson favoured chlorodyne. The conversation then turned on the deadly qualities of that drug when taken in excess, of the fatal sleep in which it lulled its victims. So disastrous were the incidents cited, that half an hour later, when, her aunt and Susan being out, Chrissie took a small bottle of chlorodyne from the mantelpiece, the boatswain implored her to try his nastier but safer remedy instead.

'Nonsense!' cried Chrissie, 'I'm only going to take twenty drops—one—two—three——"

The drug suddenly poured out in a little stream.

'I should think that's about it,' said Chrissie, holding the tumbler up to the light.

'It's about five hundred!' said the horrified Tucker. 'Don't take that, miss, whatever you do; let me measure it for you.'

The girl waved him away, and, before he could interfere, drank off the contents of the glass and resumed her seat. The boatswain watched her uneasily, and taking up the phial carefully read through the directions. After that he was not at all surprised to see the book fall from his charge's hand on to the floor, and her eyes close.

'I knew it,' said Tucker, in profuse perspiration, 'I knew it. These wretched girls are all alike. Always know what's best. Miss Polson! Miss Polson!'

He shook her roughly, but to no purpose, and then running to the door, shouted eagerly for Susan. No reply forthcoming he ran to the window, but there was nobody in sight, and he came back and stood in front of the girl, wringing his huge hands helplessly. It was a great question for a poor sailor. If he went for the doctor he deserted his post; if he didn't go his charge might die. He made one more attempt to awaken her, and, seizing a flower-glass, splashed her freely with cold water. She did not even wince.

'It's no use fooling with it,' murmured Tucker; 'I must get the doctor, that's all.'

He quitted the room, and, dashing hastily downstairs, had already opened the hall door when a thought struck him, and he came back again. Chrissie was still asleep in the chair, and, with a smile at the clever way in which he had solved a difficulty, he stooped down, and, raising her in his strong arms, bore her from the room and downstairs. Then a hitch occurred. The triumphant progress was marred by the behaviour of the hall door, which, despite his efforts, refused to be opened, and, encumbered by his fair burden, he could not for some time ascertain the reason. Then, full of shame that so much deceit could exist in so fair and frail a habitation, he discovered that Miss Polson's foot was pressing firmly against it. Her eyes were still closed and her head heavy, but the fact remained that one foot was acting in a manner that was full of intelligence and guile, and when he took it away from the door the other one took its place. By a sudden manœuvre the wily Tucker turned his back on the door, and opened it, and, at the same moment, a hand came to life again and dealt him a stinging slap on the face.

'Idiot!' said the indignant Chrissie, slipping from his arms and confronting him. 'How dare you take such a liberty?'

The astonished boatswain felt his face, and regarded her open-mouthed.

'Don't you ever dare speak to me again,' said the offended maiden, drawing herself up with irreproachable dignity. 'I am disgusted with your conduct. Most unbearable!'

'I was carrying you off to the doctor,' said the boatswain. 'How was I to know you were only shamming?'

'*Shamming?*' said Chrissie, in tones of incredulous horror. 'I was asleep. I often go to sleep in the afternoon.'

The boatswain made no reply, except to grin with great intelligence as he followed his charge upstairs again. He grinned at intervals until the return of Susan and Miss Polson, who, trying to look unconcerned, came in later on, both apparently suffering from temper, Susan especially. Amid the sympathetic interruptions of these listeners Chrissie recounted her experiences, while the boatswain, despite his better sense, felt like the greatest scoundrel unhung, a feeling which was fostered by the remarks of Susan and the chilling regards of Miss Polson.

'I shall inform the captain,' said Miss Polson, bridling. 'It's my duty.'

'Oh, I shall tell him,' said Chrissie. 'I shall tell him the moment he comes in at the door.'

'So shall I,' said Susan; 'the idea of taking such liberties!'

Having fired this broadside, the trio watched the enemy narrowly and anxiously.

'If I've done anything wrong, ladies,' said the unhappy boatswain, 'I'm sorry. I can't say anything fairer than that, and I'll tell the cap'n myself exactly how I came to do it when he comes in.'

'Pah! tell-tale!' said Susan.

'Of course, if you are here to fetch and carry,' said Miss Polson, with withering emphasis.

'The idea of a grown man telling tales,' said Chrissie scornfully. 'Baby!'

80

'Why, just now you were all going to tell him yourselves,' said the bewildered boatswain.

The two elder women rose and regarded him with looks of pitying disdain. Miss Polson's glance said 'Fool!' plainly; Susan, a simple child of nature, given to expressing her mind freely, said 'Blockhead!' with conviction.

'I see how it is,' said the boatswain, after ruminating deeply. 'Well, I won't split, ladies. I can see now you were all in it, and it was a little plan to get me out of the house.'

'What a head he has got,' said the irritated Susan; 'isn't it wonderful how he thinks of it all! Nobody would think he was so clever to look at him.'

'Still waters run deep,' said the boatswain, who was beginning to have a high opinion of himself.

'And pride goes before a fall,' said Chrissie, 'remember that, Mr Tucker.'

Mr Tucker grinned, but, remembering the fable of the pitcher and the well, pressed his superior officer that evening to relieve him of his duties. He stated that the strain was slowly undermining a constitution which was not so strong as appearances would warrant, and that his knowledge of female nature was lamentably deficient on many important points.

'You're doing very well,' said the captain, who had no intention of attending any more charitable meetings, 'very well indeed; I am proud of you.'

'It isn't a man's work,' objected the boatswain. 'Besides, if anything happens you'll blame me for it.'

'Nothing can happen,' declared the captain confidently. 'We shall make a start in about four days now. You're the only man I can trust with such a difficult job, Tucker, and I shan't forget you.'

'Very good,' said the other dejectedly. 'I obey orders then.'

The next day passed quietly, the members of the household making a great fuss of Tucker, and thereby filling him with forebodings of the worst possible nature. On the day after, when the captain, having business at a neighbouring town, left him in sole change, his uneasiness could not be concealed.

'I'm going for a walk,' said Chrissie, as he sat by himself, working out dangerous moves and the best means of checking them; 'would you care to come with me, Tucker?'

'I wish you wouldn't put it that way, miss,' said the boatswain, as he reached for his hat.

'I want exercise,' said Chrissie; 'I've been cooped up long enough.'

She set off at a good pace up the High Street, attended by her faithful follower, and passing through the small suburbs, struck out into the country beyond. After four miles the boatswain, who was no walker, reminded her that they had got to go back.

'Plenty of time,' said Chrissie, 'we have got the day before us. Isn't it glorious? Do you see that milestone, Tucker, I'll race you to it; come along.'

She was off on the instant, with the boatswain, who suspected treachery, after her.

'You *can* run,' she panted, thoughtfully, as she came in second; 'we'll have another one presently. You don't know how good it is for you, Tucker.'

The boatswain grinned sourly and looked at her from the corner of his eye. The next three miles passed like a horrible nightmare; his charge making a race of every milestone, in which the labouring boatswain, despite his want of practice, came in the winner. The fourth ended disastrously, Chrissie limping the last ten yards, and seating herself with a very woebegone face on the stone itself.

'You did very well, miss,' said the boatswain, who thought he could afford to be generous. 'You needn't be offended about it.'

'It's my ankle,' said Chrissie with a little whimper. 'Oh! I twisted it right round.'

The boatswain stood regarding her in silent consternation.

'It's no use looking like that,' said Chrissie sharply, 'you great clumsy thing. If you hadn't run so hard it wouldn't have happened. It's all your fault.'

'If you don't mind leaning on me a bit,' said Tucker, 'we might get along.'

Chrissie took his arm petulantly, and they started on their return journey, at the rate of about four hours a mile, with little cries and gasps at every yard.

'It's no use,' said Chrissie as she relinquished his arm, and, limping to the side of the road, sat down. The boatswain pricked up his ears hopefully at the sound of approaching wheels.

'What's the matter with the young lady?' inquired a groom who was driving a little trap, as he pulled up and regarded with interest a grimace of extraordinary intensity on the young lady's face.

'Broke her ankle, I think,' said the boatswain glibly. 'Which way are you going?'

'Well, I'm going to Barborough,' said the groom; 'but my guvnor's rather particular.'

'I'll make it all right with you,' said the boatswain.

The groom hesitated a minute, and then made way for Chrissie as the boatswain assisted her to get up beside him; then Tucker, with a grin of satisfaction at getting a seat once more, clambered up behind, and they started.

'Have a rug, mate,' said the groom, handing the reins to Chrissie and passing it over; 'put it round your knees and tuck the ends under you.'

'Ay, ay, mate,' said the boatswain as he obeyed the instructions.

'Are you sure you are quite comfortable?' said the groom affectionately.

'Quite,' said the other.

The groom said no more, but in a quiet business-like

fashion placed his hands on the seaman's broad back and shot him out into the road. Then he snatched up the reins and drove off at a gallop.

Without the faintest hope of winning, Mr Tucker, who realized clearly, appearances notwithstanding, that he had fallen into a trap, rose after a hurried rest and started on his fifth race that morning. The prize was only a second-rate groom with plated buttons, who was waving cheery farewells to him with a dingy top hat; but the boatswain would have sooner had it than a silver tea-service.

He ran as he had never run before in his life, but all to no purpose, the trap stopping calmly a little farther on to take up another passenger, in whose favour the groom retired to the back seat; then, with a final wave of the hand to him, they took a road to the left and drove rapidly out of sight. The boatswain's watch was over.

In Mid-Atlantic

'NO sir,' said the night-watchman, as he took a seat on a post at the end of the jetty, and stowed a huge piece of tobacco in his cheek. 'No, man and boy I was at sea for forty years before I took on this job, but I can't say that I ever saw a real, downright ghost.'

This was disappointing, and I said so. Previous experience of the power of Bill's vision had led me to expect something very different.

'Not but what I've known some queer things happen,' said Bill, fixing his eyes on the Surrey side, and going off into a kind of trance. 'Queer things.'

I waited patiently; Bill's eyes, after resting for some time on Surrey, began slowly to cross the river, paused midway in reasonable hopes of a collision between a tug with its flotilla of barges and a penny steamer, and then came back to me.

'You heard that yarn old Cap'n Harris was telling the other day about the skipper he knew having a warning one night to alter his course, and doing so, picked up five live men and three dead bodies in an open boat?' he inquired.

I nodded.

'The yarn in various forms is an old one,' said I.

'It's all founded on something I told him once,' said Bill. 'I don't wish to accuse Cap'n Harris of taking another man's true story and spoiling it; he's got a bad memory, that's all. First of all, he forgets he ever heard the yarn; secondly, he goes and spoils it.'

I gave a sympathetic murmur. Harris was as truthful an old man as ever breathed, but his tales were terribly restricted by this circumstance, whereas Bill's were limited by nothing but his own imagination.

'It was about fifteen years ago now,' began Bill, getting the quid of tobacco into a by-way of his cheek, where it would not impede his utterance. 'I was A.B. on the *Swallow*, a barque, trading wherever we could pick up stuff. On this voyage we were bound from London to Jamaica with a general cargo.

'The start of the voyage was excellent. We were towed out of the St Katherine's Docks here, to the Nore, and the tug left us to a stiff breeze, which fairly raced us down Channel and out into the Atlantic. Everybody was saying what a fine voyage we were having, and what quick time we should make, and the first mate was in such a lovely temper that you might do almost anything with him.

'We were about ten days out, and still slipping along in this spanking way, when all of a sudden things changed. I was at the wheel with the second mate one night, when the skipper, whose name was Brown, came up from below in an uneasy sort of fashion, and stood looking at us for some time without speaking. Then at last he sort of makes up his mind, and says he:

'"Mr McMillan, I've just had a most remarkable experience, and I don't know what to do about it."

'"Yes, sir?" says Mr McMillan.

'"Three times I've been woken during the night by something shouting in my ear, 'Steer nor'-nor'-west!'" says the captain very solemnly, "'Steer nor'-nor'-west!' that's all it says. The first time I thought it was somebody who'd got into my cabin skylarking, and I laid about with a stick, but I've heard it three times, and there's nothing there."

'"It's a supernatural warning," says the second mate, who had a great uncle once who had the second sight, and was the most unpopular man of his family, because he always knew what to expect, and laid his plans accordingly.

'"That's what I think," says the cap'n. "There's some poor shipwrecked fellow creatures in distress."

'"It's a verra grave responsebeelity," says Mr McMillan. "I should just ca' up the fairst mate."

'"Bill," says the Cap'n, "just go below, and tell Mr Salmon I'd like a few words with him particularly."

'Well, I went down below, and called up the first mate, and as soon as I'd explained to him what he was wanted for, he went right off into a fit of outrageous bad language. He came right up on deck without being properly dressed. A most disrespectful way to come to the cap'n, but he was so hot and excited that he didn't care what he did.

'"Mr Salmon," says the cap'n gravely, "I've just had a most solemn warning, and I want to——"

'"I know," says the mate gruffly.

'"What! have you heard it too?" says the cap'n, in surprise. "Three times?"

'"I heard it from him," says the mate, pointing to me. "Nightmare, sir, nightmare."

'"It was not a nightmare, sir," says the cap'n very huffily, "and if I hear it again, I'm going to alter this ship's course."

'Well, the first mate was in a hole. He wanted to call the skipper something which he knew wasn't discipline. I knew what it was, and I knew if the mate didn't do something he'd be ill, he was that sort of man, everything flew to his head. He walked away, and put his head over the side for a bit, and at last, when he came back, he was comparatively calm.

'"You mustn't hear those words again, sir," says he; "don't

go to sleep again tonight. Stay up, and we'll have a hand of cards. Don't spoil one of the best trips we've ever had," says he, in a pleading manner.

'"Mr Salmon," says the cap'n, very angry, "I shall not fly in the face of Providence in any such way. I shall sleep as usual."

'Well, Mr Salmon, who was getting very mad, stalks down below, followed by the cap'n, and Mr McMillan was so excited that he even started talking to me about it. Half an hour afterwards the cap'n came running up on deck again.

'"Mr McMillan," says he excitedly, "steer nor'-nor'-west until further orders. I've heard it again, and this time it nearly split the drum of my ear."

'The ship's course was altered, and after the old man was satisfied he went back to bed again, and almost directly after this eight bells went, and I was relieved. I wasn't on deck when the first mate came up, but those who were said he took it very calmly. He didn't say a word. He just sat down on the poop, and blew his cheeks out.

'As soon as ever it was daylight the skipper was on deck with his glasses. He sent men up to the masthead to keep a good look-out, and he was dancing about like a cat on hot bricks all the morning.

'"How long are we to go on this course, sir?" asks Mr Salmon, about ten o'clock in the morning.

'"I've not made up my mind, sir," says the cap'n, very stately; but I could see he was looking a trifle foolish.

'At twelve o'clock in the day, the first mate got a cough, and every time he coughed it seemed to act upon the skipper, and made him madder and madder. Now that it was broad daylight, Mr McMillan didn't seem to be so creepy as the night before, and I could see the cap'n was only waiting for the slightest excuse to get into our proper course again.

'"That's a nasty, bad cough of yours, Mr Salmon," says he, eyeing the mate very hard.

'"Yes, a nasty, irritating sort of cough, sir," says the other; "it worries me a great deal. It's this going up nor'ards that's sticking in my throat," says he.

'The cap'n gives a gulp, and walks off, but he comes back in a minute, and says he:

'"Mr Salmon, I should think it a great pity to lose a valuable officer like yourself, even to do good to others. There's a hard ring about that cough I don't like, and if you really think it's going up this bit north, why, I don't mind putting the ship in her course again."

'Well, the mate thanked him kindly, and he was just about to give the orders when one of the men who was at the masthead suddenly shouts out:

'"Ahoy! Small boat on the port bow!"

'The cap'n started as if he'd been shot, and ran up the rigging with his glasses. He came down again almost directly, and his face was all in a glow with pleasure and excitement.

'"Mr Salmon," says he, "here's a small boat with a lug sail in the middle of the Atlantic, with one poor man lying in the bottom of her. What do you think of my warning now?'

'"The mate didn't say anything at first, but he took the glasses and had a look, and when he came back anyone could see his opinion of the skipper had gone up miles and miles.

'"It's a wonderful thing, sir," says he, "and one I'll remember all my life. It's evident that you've been picked out as an instrument to do this good work."

'I'd never heard the first mate talk like that before, 'cept once when he fell overboard and was stuck in the Thames mud. He said that was Providence; though, as it was low water, according to the tide-table, I couldn't see what Providence had to do with it myself. He was as excited as anybody, and took the wheel himself, and put the ship's head for the boat, and as she came closer, our boat was slung out, and the second mate and I and three other men dropped into her, and pulled in the direction of the other.

'"Never mind the boat; we don't want to be bothered with her," shouts out the cap'n as we pulled away—"Save the man!"

'I'll say this for Mr McMillan, he steered that boat beautifully, and we ran alongside of the other as easily as was possible. Two of us shipped our oars, and gripped her tightly, and then we saw that she was just an ordinary boat, partly decked in, with the head and shoulders of a man showing in the opening, fast asleep and snoring like thunder.

'"Puir chap," says Mr McMillan, standing up. "Look how wasted he is."

'He took hold of the man by the neck of his coat and his belt, and, being a very powerful man, dragged him up and swung him into our boat, which was bobbing up and down, and grating against the side of the other. We let go then, and the man we'd rescued opened his eyes as Mr McMillan tumbled over one of the thwarts with him, and, letting off a roar like a bull, tried to jump back into his boat.

'"Hold him!" shouted the second mate. "Hold him tight! He's mad, puir fellow."

'By the way that man fought and yelled, we thought the mate was right, too. He was a short, stiff chap, hard as iron, and he bit and kicked and swore for all he was worth, until at last we tripped him up and tumbled him into the bottom of the boat, and held him there with his head hanging over a thwart.

'"It's all right, my puir fellow," says the second mate; "ye're in good hands—ye're saved."

'"What's your little game?" says the man. "Where's my boat—eh? Where's my boat?"

'He wriggled a bit, and got his head up, and, when he saw it bowling along two or three hundred yards away, his temper got the better of him, and he swore that if Mr McMillan didn't row after it he'd knife him.

'"We can't bother about the boat," says the mate; "we've had enough bother to rescue you."

90

'"Who the dickens wanted you to rescue me?" bellowed the man. "I'll make you pay for this, you miserable swabs. If there's any law in America you shall have it!"

'By this time we had got to the ship, which had shortened sail, and the cap'n was standing by the side, looking down upon the stranger with a big, kind smile which nearly sent him crazy.

'"Welcome aboard, my poor fellow," says he, holding out his hand as the chap got up the side.

'"Are you the author of this outrage?" says the man fiercely.

'"I don't understand you," says the cap'n in a very dignified manner, drawing himself up.

'"Did you send your chaps to sneak me out of my boat while I was having forty winks?" roars the other.

'"Surely," says the cap'n, "surely you didn't wish to be left to perish in that little craft. I had a supernatural warning to steer this course on purpose to pick you up, and this is your gratitude."

'"Look here!" says the other. "My name's Cap'n Naskett, and I'm doing a record trip from New York to Liverpool in the smallest boat that has ever crossed the Atlantic, and you go and mess up everything with your cussed officiousness. If you think I'm going to be kidnapped just to fulfil your beastly warnings, you've made a mistake. I'll have the law on you, that's what I'll do. Kidnapping's a punishable offence."

'"What did you come here for, then?" says the cap'n.

'"Come!" howls Cap'n Naskett. "Come! A fellow sneaks up alongside of me with a boat-load of street-sweepings dressed as sailors, and snaps me up while I'm asleep, and you ask me why I came. Look here. You clap on all sail and catch that boat of mine, and put me back, and I'll call it quits. If you don't, I'll bring a law-suit against you, and make you the laughing-stock of two continents into the bargain."

'Well, to make the best of a bad bargain, the cap'n sailed

after the cussed little boat, and Mr Salmon, who thought more than enough time had been lost already, fell foul of Cap'n Naskett. They were both pretty talkers, and the way they went on was an education for every sailorman afloat. Every man aboard got as near as they dare to listen to them; but I must say Cap'n Naskett had the best of it. He was a sarcastic man, and pretended to think the ship was fitted out just to pick up shipwrecked people, and he also pretended to think we were castaways who had been saved by it. He said of course anybody could see at a glance we weren't sailormen, and he supposed Mr Salmon was a butcher who had been carried out to sea while paddling at Margate to strengthen his ankles.

'He said a lot more of this sort of thing, and all this time we were chasing his miserable little boat, and he was admiring the way she sailed, while the first mate was answering his taunts, and I'm sure that not even the skipper was more pleased than Mr Salmon when we caught it up at last, and shoved him back. He was ungrateful up to the last, and just before leaving the ship, actually went up to Cap'n Brown and advised him to shut his eyes and turn round three times and catch what he could.

'I never saw the skipper so upset before, but I heard him tell Mr McMillan that night that if he ever went out of his way again after a craft, it would only be to run it down. Most people keep pretty quiet about supernatural things that happen to them, but he was about the quietest I ever heard of, and what's more, he made everyone else keep quiet about it too. Even when he had to steer nor'-nor'-west after that, in the normal course of business, he didn't like it, and he was about the most cruelly disappointed man you ever saw when he heard afterwards that Cap'n Naskett got safely to Liverpool.'

After the Inquest

IT was a fair evening in late summer in the parish of Wapping. The hands had long since left, and the night-watchman having abandoned his trust in favour of a neighbouring bar, the wharf was deserted.

An elderly seaman came to the gate and paused irresolute, then, seeing all was quiet, stole cautiously on the jetty, and stood for some time gazing curiously down on to the deck of the flat-bottomed, sloop-rigged *Pscyche*, lying alongside.

With the exception of the mate, who, since the lamented disappearance of its late master and owner, was acting as captain, the deck was as deserted as the wharf. He was smoking an evening pipe in all the pride of a first command, his eye roving fondly from the blunt bows and untidy deck of his craft to her clumsy stern, when a slight cough from the man above attracted his attention.

'How do, George?' said the man on the jetty, somewhat sheepishly, as the other looked up.

The mate opened his mouth, and his pipe fell from it and smashed to pieces unnoticed.

'Got much stuff in her this trip?' continued the man, with an obvious attempt to appear at ease.

The mate, still looking up, backed slowly to the other side of the deck, but made no reply.

'What's the matter, man?' said the other testily. 'You don't seem overpleased to see me.'

He leaned over as he spoke, and, laying hold of the rigging, descended to the deck, while the mate took his breath in short, exhilarating gasps.

'Here I am, George,' said the intruder, 'turned up like a bad penny, and glad to see your handsome face again, I can tell you.'

In response to this flattering remark George gurgled.

'Why,' said the other, with an uneasy laugh, 'did you think I was dead, George? Ha, Ha! Feel that!'

He gave the horrified man a thump in the back, which stopped even his gurgles.

'That feel like a dead man?' asked the smiter, raising his hand again. 'Feel——'

The mate moved back hastily. 'That'll do,' said he fiercely; 'ghost or no ghost, don't you hit me like that again.'

'All right, George,' said the other, as he meditatively felt the stiff grey whiskers which framed his face. 'What's the news?'

'The news,' said George, who was of slow habits and speech, 'is that you were found last Tuesday week off St Katherine's Stairs, the inquest was held on Friday week at the Town of Ramsgate public-house, and you were buried on Monday afternoon at Lowestoft.'

'Buried?' gasped the other, 'inquest? You've been drinking, George.'

'And a pretty penny your funeral cost, I can tell you,' continued the mate. 'There's a headstone being made now—"Lived lamented and died respected", I think it is, with "Not lost, but gone before", at the bottom.'

'Lived respected and died lamented, you mean,' growled the old man; 'well, a nice muddle you have made of it between you. Things always go wrong when I'm not here to look after them.'

'You aren't dead, then?' said the mate, taking no notice of this unreasonable remark. 'Where've you been all this long time?'

'No more than you're master of this ship,' replied Mr Harbolt grimly. 'I—I've been a bit queer in the stomach, and I took a little drink to correct it. Foolishly, I took the wrong drink, and it must have got into my head.'

'That's the worst of not being used to it,' said the mate, without moving a muscle.

The skipper eyed him solemnly, but the mate stood firm.

'After that,' continued the skipper, still watching him suspiciously, 'I remember no more distinctly until this morning, when I found myself sitting on a step down Poplar way and shivering, with the morning newspaper and a crowd around me.'

'Morning newspaper!' repeated the mystified mate. 'What was that for?'

'Decency. I was wrapped up in it,' replied the skipper. 'Where I came from or how I got there I don't know. I suppose I must have been ill; I seem to remember taking something out of a bottle pretty often. Some old gentleman in the crowd took me into a shop and bought me these clothes, and here I am. My own clothes and thirty pounds of freight money I had in my pocket are all gone.'

'Well, I'm very glad to see you back,' said the mate. 'It's quite a home-coming for you, too. Your wife is down aft.'

'My wife? What's she aboard for?' growled the skipper, successfully controlling his natural gratification at the news.

'She's been with us for the last two trips,' replied the mate. 'She's had business to settle in London, and she's been going through your lockers to clear up.'

'My lockers!' groaned the skipper. 'Good heavens! there are things in those lockers I wouldn't have her see for the

95

world; women are so fussy and so fond of making something out of nothing. There's a poor female touched a bit in the head, who's been writing love-letters to me, George.'

'Three poor females,' said the precise mate; 'your wife has got all the letters tied up with blue ribbon. Very far gone they were, too, poor creatures.'

'George,' said the skipper in a broken voice, 'I'm a ruined man. I'll never hear the end of this. I guess I'll go and sleep for'ard this voyage and lie low. Be careful you don't let on I'm aboard, and after she's home I'll take the ship again, and let the thing leak out gradually. Come to life bit by bit, so to speak. It wouldn't do to scare her, George; in the meantime I'll try and think of some explanation to give her. You might be thinking too.'

'I'll do what I can,' said the mate.

'Crack me up to the old girl all you can; tell her I used to write to all sorts of people when I got a drop of drink in me; say how thoughtful I always was of her. You might tell her about that gold locket I bought for her, which someone robbed me of.'

'Gold locket?' said the mate in tones of great surprise. 'What gold locket? First I've heard of it.'

'Any gold locket,' said the skipper irritably; 'anything you can think of; you needn't be particular. After that you can drop little hints about people being buried in mistake for others, to prepare her a bit—I don't want to scare her.'

'Leave it to me,' said the mate.

'I'll go and turn in now, I'm dead tired,' said the skipper. 'I suppose Joe and the boy's asleep?'

George nodded, and meditatively watched the other as he pushed back the fore-scuttle and drew it after him as he descended. Then a thought struck the mate, and he ran hastily forward and threw his weight on the scuttle just in time to frustrate the efforts of Joe and the boy, who were coming on deck to tell him a new ghost story. The confusion below was frightful, the skipper's cry of 'It's only me, Joe,' not possessing the soothing effect which he intended. They calmed down at length, after their visitor had convinced them that he really was flesh and blood and fists, and the boy's attention being directed to a small rug in the corner of the fo'c'sle, the skipper took his bunk and was soon fast asleep.

He slept so soundly that the noise of the vessel getting under way failed to rouse him, and she was well out in the open river when he awoke, and after cautiously protruding his head through the scuttle, ventured on deck. For some time he stood eagerly sniffing the cool, sweet air, and then, after a look round, gingerly approached the mate, who was at the helm.

'Give me hold of her,' said he.

'You'd better get below again, if you don't want your wife to see you,' said the mate. 'She's getting up—nasty temper she's in too.'

The skipper went forward grumbling. 'Send down a good breakfast, George,' said he.

To his great discomfort the mate suddenly gave a low whistle, and regarded him with a look of blank dismay.

'Good gracious!' he cried, 'I forgot all about it. Here's a pretty kettle of fish—well, well.'

'Forgot about what?' asked the skipper uneasily.

'The crew take their meals in the cabin now,' replied the mate, ''cos your wife says it's more cheerful for them, and she's teaching them to eat their food properly.'

The skipper looked at him aghast. 'You'll have to smuggle me some food,' he said at length. 'I'm not going to starve for anybody.'

'Easier said than done,' said the mate. 'Your wife has got eyes like needles; still, I'll do the best I can for you. Look out! Here she comes.'

The skipper fled hastily, and, safe down below, explained to the crew how they were to secrete portions of their breakfast for his benefit. The amount of explanation required for so simple a matter was remarkable, the crew manifesting a denseness which irritated him almost beyond endurance. They promised, however, to do the best they could for him, and returned in triumph after a hearty meal, and presented their enraged commander with a few greasy crumbs and the tail of a bloater.

For the next two days the wind was against them, and they made but little progress. Mrs Harbolt spent most of her time on deck, thereby confining her husband to his evil-smelling quarters below. Matters were not improved for him by his treatment of the crew, who, resenting his rough treatment of them, were doing their best to starve him into civility. Most of the time he kept in his bunk—or rather Jemmy's bunk—a prey to despondency and hunger of an acute type, venturing on deck only at night to prowl uneasily about and bemoan his condition.

On the third night Mrs Harbolt was later in retiring than usual, and it was nearly midnight before the skipper, who had been indignantly waiting for her to go, was able to get on deck and hold counsel with the mate.

'I've done what I could for you,' said the latter, fishing a crust from his pocket, which Harbolt took thankfully. 'I've told her all the yarns I could think of about people turning up after they were buried and so forth.'

'What'd she say?' queried the skipper eagerly, between his bites.

'Told me not to talk like that,' said the mate; 'said it showed a want of trust in Providence to hint at such things. Then I told her what you asked me about the locket, only I made it a bracelet worth ten pounds.'

'That pleased her?' suggested the other hopefully.

The mate shook his head. 'She said I was a born fool to believe you'd been robbed of it,' he replied. 'She said what

98

you'd done was to give it to one of those poor females. She's been going on frightfully about it all afternoon—won't talk of anything else.'

'I don't know what's to be done,' groaned the skipper despondently. 'I shall be dead before we get to port if this wind holds. Go down and get me something to eat, George; I'm starving.'

'Everything's locked up, as I told you before,' said the mate.

'As the master of this ship,' said the skipper, drawing himself up, 'I order you to go down and get me something to eat. You can tell my wife it's for you if she says anything.'

'I'm hanged if I will,' said the mate sturdily. 'Why don't you go down and have it out with her like a man? She can't eat you.'

'I'm not going to,' said the other shortly. 'I'm a determined man, and when I say a thing I mean it. It's going to be broken to her gradually, as I said; I don't want her to be scared, poor thing.'

'I know who'd be scared the most,' murmured the mate.

The skipper looked at him fiercely, then sat down wearily on the hatches with his hands between his knees, rising after a time, to get the dipper and drink copiously from the water-cask. Then, replacing it with a sigh, he bade the mate a surly good night and went below.

To his dismay he found when he awoke in the morning that what little wind there was had dropped in the night, and the vessel was just rising and falling lazily on the water in a fashion most objectionable to an empty stomach. It was the last straw, and he made things so uncomfortable below that the crew were glad to escape on deck, where they squatted down in the bows and proceeded to review a situation which was rapidly becoming unbearable.

'I've had enough of it, Joe,' grumbled the boy. 'I'm sore all over with sleeping on the floor, and the old man's temper gets worse and worse. I'm going to be ill.'

'What for?' queried Joe dully.

'You tell the cap'n's wife I'm down below ill. Say you think I'm dying,' responded the infant Machiavelli, 'then you'll see something if you keep your eyes open.'

He went below again, not without a little nervousness, and, clambering into Joe's bunk, rolled over on his back and gave a deep groan.

'What's the matter with *you*?' growled the skipper, who was lying in the other bunk staving off the pangs of hunger with a pipe.

'I'm very ill—dying,' said Jemmy, with another groan.

'You'd better stay in bed and have your breakfast brought down here, then,' said the skipper kindly.

'I don't want any breakfast,' said Jemmy faintly.

'That's no reason why you shouldn't have it sent down, you unfeeling little brute,' said the skipper indignantly. 'You tell Joe to bring you down a great plate of cold meat and pickles, and some coffee; that's what you want.'

'All right, sir,' said Jemmy. 'I hope they won't let your wife come down here, in case it's something catching. I wouldn't like her to be taken bad.'

'Eh?' said the skipper, in alarm. 'Certainly not. Here, you go up and die on deck. Hurry up with you.'

'I can't; I'm too weak,' said Jemmy.

'You get up on deck at once; d'you hear me?' hissed the skipper in alarm.

'I c-c-c-can't help it,' sobbed Jemmy, who was enjoying the situation amazingly. 'I believe it's sleeping on the hard floor's snapped something inside me.'

'If you don't go I'll take you,' said the skipper, and he was about to rise to put his threat into execution when a shadow fell across the opening, and a voice, which thrilled him to the core, said softly, 'Jemmy!'

'Yes'm?' said Jemmy languidly, as the skipper flattened himself in his bunk and drew the clothes over him.

'How do you feel?' inquired Mrs Harbolt.

'Bad all over,' said Jemmy. 'Oh, don't come down, mum—please don't.'

'Rubbish!' said Mrs Harbolt tartly, as she came slowly and carefully down backwards. 'What a dark hole this is, Jemmy. No wonder you're ill. Put your tongue out.'

Jemmy complied.

'I can't see properly here,' murmured the lady, 'but it looks very large. Suppose you go in the other bunk, Jemmy. It's a good bit higher than this, and you'd get more air and be more comfortable altogether.'

'Joe wouldn't like it, mum,' said the boy anxiously. The last glimpse he had had of the skipper's face did not make him yearn to share his bed with him.

'Stuff and nonsense!' said Mrs Harbolt hotly. 'Who's Joe, I'd like to know? Out you come.'

'I can't move, mum,' said Jemmy firmly.

'Nonsense!' said the lady. 'I'll just put it straight for you first, then in it you go.'

'No don't, mum,' shouted Jemmy, now thoroughly alarmed at the success of his plot. 'There, there's a gentleman in that bunk. A gentleman we brought from London for a change of sea air.'

'My goodness gracious!' ejaculated the surprised Mrs Harbolt. 'I never did. Why, what's he had to eat?'

'He—he—didn't want anything to eat,' said Jemmy, with a woeful disregard for facts.

'What's the matter with him?' inquired Mrs Harbolt, eyeing the bunk curiously. 'What's his name? Who is he?'

'He's been lost a long time,' said Jemmy, 'and he's forgotten who he is—he's an oldish man with a red face and a little white whisker all round it—a very nice-looking man, I mean,' he interposed hurriedly. 'I don't think he's quite right in the head, because he says he ought to have been buried instead of someone else. Oh!'

The last word was almost a scream, for Mrs Harbolt, staggering back, pinched him convulsively.

'Jemmy!' she gasped, in a trembling voice, as she suddenly remembered certain mysterious hints thrown out by the mate. 'Who is it?'

'The *captain*!' said Jemmy, and, breaking from her clasp, slipped from his bed and darted hastily on deck, just as the pallid face of his commander broke through the blankets and beamed anxiously on his wife.

Five minutes later, as the crew gathered aft were curiously eyeing the fo'c'sle, Mrs Harbolt and the skipper came on deck. To the great astonishment of the mate, the eyes of the redoubtable woman were slightly wet, and, regardless of the presence of the men, she clung fondly to her husband as they walked slowly to the cabin. Before they went below, however, she called the grinning Jemmy to her, and, to his private grief and public shame, tucked his head under her arm and kissed him fondly.

In Limehouse Reach

IT was the mate's affair all through. He began by leaving the end of a line dangling over the stern, and the propeller, though quite unaccustomed to that sort of work, wound it up until only a few fathoms remained. It then stopped, and the mischief was not discovered until the skipper had called the engineer everything that he and the mate and three men and a boy could think of. The skipper did the interpreting through the tube which afforded the sole means of communication between the wheel and the engine-room, and the indignant engineer did the listening.

The *Gem* was just off Limehouse at the time, and it was evident she was going to stay there. The skipper ran her ashore and made her fast to a roomy old schooner which was lying alongside a wharf. He was then able to give a little attention to the real offender, and the unfortunate mate, who had been the most inventive of them all, realized to the full the old saying of curses coming home to roost. They brought some strangers with them, too.

'I'm going ashore,' said the skipper at last. 'We won't get off till next tide now. When it's low water you'll have to get down and cut the line away. A new line too! I'm ashamed of you, Harry.'

'I'm not surprised,' said the engineer, who was a vindictive man.

'What do you mean by that?' demanded the mate fiercely.

'We don't want any of your bad temper,' interposed the skipper severely. '*Nor* bad language. The men can go ashore, and the engineer too, provided he keeps steam up. But be ready to start about five. You'll have to mind the ship.'

He looked over the stern again, shook his head sadly, and, after a visit to the cabin, clambered over the schooner's side and got ashore. The men, after looking at the propeller and shaking their heads, went ashore too, and the boy, after looking at the propeller and getting ready to shake his, caught the mate's eye and omitted that part of the ceremony, from a sudden conviction that it was unhealthy.

Left alone, the mate, who was of a sensitive disposition, after a curt nod to Captain Jansell of the schooner *Aquila*, who had heard of the disaster, and was disposed to be sympathetically inquisitive, lit his pipe and began moodily to smoke.

When he next looked up the old man had disappeared, and a girl in a print dress and a large straw hat sat in a wicker chair reading. She was such a pretty girl that the mate forgot his troubles at once, and, after carefully putting his cap on straight, strolled casually up and down the deck.

To his mortification, the girl seemed unaware of his presence, and read steadily, occasionally looking up and chirping with a pair of ravishing lips at a bird which hung in a wicker cage from the mainmast.

'That's a nice bird,' said the mate, leaning against the side, and turning a look of great admiration upon it.

'Yes,' said the girl, raising a pair of dark blue eyes to the bold brown ones, and taking him in at a glance.

'Does it sing?' inquired the mate, with a show of great interest.

104

'It does sometimes, when we are alone,' was the reply.

'I should have thought the sea air would have affected its throat,' said the mate, reddening. 'Are you often in the London river, miss? I don't seem to remember seeing your craft before.'

'Not often,' said the girl.

'You've got a fine schooner here,' said the mate, eyeing it critically. 'For my part, I prefer a sailer to a steamer.'

'I should think you would,' said the girl.

'Why?' inquired the mate tenderly, pleased at this show of interest.

'No propeller,' said the girl quietly, and she left her seat and disappeared below, leaving the mate gasping painfully.

Left to himself, he became melancholy, as he realized that the great passion of his life had commenced, and would probably end in a few hours. The engineer came aboard to look at the fires, and, the steamer being now on the soft mud, good-naturedly went down and assisted him to free the propeller before going ashore again. Then he was alone once more, gazing ruefully at the bare deck of the *Aquila*.

It was past two o'clock in the afternoon before any signs of life other than the bird appeared there. Then the girl came on deck again, accompanied by a stout woman of middle age, and an appearance so affable that the mate commenced at once.

'Fine day,' he said pleasantly, as he brought up in front of them.

'Lovely weather,' said the mother, settling herself in her chair and putting down her work ready for a chat. 'I hope the wind lasts; we start tomorrow morning's tide. You'll get off this afternoon, I suppose.'

'About five o'clock,' said the mate.

'I should like to try a steamer for a change,' said the mother, and waxed garrulous on sailing craft generally, and her own in particular.

'There's five of us down there, with my husband and the two boys,' said she, indicating the cabin with her thumb; 'naturally it gets rather stuffy.'

The mate sighed. He was thinking that under some conditions there were worse things than stuffy cabins.

'And Nancy's so discontented,' said her mother, looking at the girl who was reading quietly by her side. 'She doesn't like ships or sailors. She gets her head turned reading those penny novelettes.'

'You look after your own head,' said Nancy elegantly, without looking up.

'Girls in those novels don't talk to *their* mothers like that,' said the elder woman severely.

'They have different sorts of mothers,' said Nancy, serenely turning over a page. 'I hate little pokey ships and sailors smelling of tar. I never saw a sailor I liked yet.'

The mate's face fell. 'There's sailors and sailors,' he suggested humbly.

'It's no good talking to her,' said the mother, with a look of fat resignation on her face, 'we can only let her go her own way; if you talked to her twenty-four hours right off it wouldn't do her any good.'

'I'd like to try,' said the mate, plucking up spirit.

'Would you?' said the girl, for the first time raising her head and looking him full in the face. 'Impudence!'

'Perhaps you haven't seen many ships,' said the impressionable mate, his eyes devouring her face. 'Would you like to come and have a look at our cabin?'

'No, thanks!' said the girl sharply. Then she smiled maliciously. 'I daresay mother would, though; she's fond of poking her nose into other people's business.'

The mother regarded her irreverent offspring fixedly for a few moments. The mate interposed.

'I should be very pleased to show you over, ma'am,' he said politely.

The mother hesitated; then she rose, and accepting the mate's assistance, clambered on to the side of the steamer, and, supported by his arms, sprang to the deck and followed him below.

'Very nice,' she said, nodding approvingly, as the mate did the honours. 'Very nice.'

'It's nice and roomy for a little craft like ours,' said the mate, as he drew a stone bottle from a locker and poured out a couple of glasses of stout. 'Try a little beer, ma'am.'

'What you must think of that girl of mine I can't think,' murmured the lady, taking a modest draught.

'The young,' said the mate, who had not quite reached his twenty-fifth year, 'are often like that.'

'It spoils her,' said the mother. 'She's a good-looking girl, too, in her way.'

'I don't see how she can help being that,' said the mate.

'Oh, get away with you,' said the lady pleasantly. 'She'll get fat like me as she gets older.'

'She couldn't do better,' said the mate tenderly.

'Nonsense,' said the lady, smiling.

'You're as like as two peas,' persisted the mate. 'I made sure you were sisters when I saw you first.'

'You aren't the first who's thought that,' said the other, laughing softly; 'not by a lot.'

'I like to see ladies about,' said the mate, who was trying desperately for a return invitation. 'I wish you could always sit there. You quite brighten the cabin up.'

'You're a flatterer,' said his visitor, as he replenished her glass, and showed so little signs of making a move that the mate, making a pretext of seeing the engineer, hurried up on deck to singe his wings once more.

'Still reading?' he said softly, as he came abreast of the girl. 'All about love, I suppose.'

'Have you left my mother down there all by herself?' inquired the girl abruptly.

'Just a minute,' said the mate, somewhat crestfallen. 'I just came up to see the engineer.'

'Well, he isn't here,' was the discouraging reply.

The mate waited a minute or two, the girl still reading quietly, and then walked back to the cabin. The sound of gentle regular breathing reached his ears, and, stepping softly, he saw to his joy that his visitor slept.

'She's asleep,' he said, going back, 'and she looks so comfortable I don't think I'll wake her.'

'I shouldn't advise you to,' said the girl; 'she always wakes up cross.'

'How strange we should run up against each other like this,' said the mate sentimentally; 'it looks like Providence, doesn't it?'

'Looks like carelessness,' said the girl.

'I don't care,' said the mate. 'I'm glad I did let that line go overboard. Best day's work I ever did. I shouldn't have seen you if I hadn't.'

'And I don't suppose you'll ever see me again,' said the girl comfortably, 'so I don't see what good you've done yourself.'

'I shall run down to Limehouse every time we're in port, anyway,' said the mate; 'it'll be odd if I don't see you sometimes. Perhaps in the night,' he added gloomily.

'I shall sit up all night watching for you,' declared Miss Jansell untruthfully.

In this cheerful fashion the conversation proceeded, the girl, who was by no means insensible to his bright eager face and well-knit figure, dividing her time in the ratio of three parts to her book and one to him. Time passed all too soon for the mate, when they were interrupted by a series of hoarse unintelligible roars proceeding from the schooner's cabin.

'That's Father,' said Miss Jansell, rising with a celerity which spoke well for the discipline maintained on the *Aquila*; 'he wants me to mend his waistcoat for him.'

She put down her book and left, the mate watching her until she disappeared down the companion way. Then he sat down and waited.

One by one the crew returned to the steamer, but the schooner's deck showed no signs of life. Then the skipper came, and, having peered critically over his vessel's side, gave orders to get under way.

'If she'd only come up,' said the miserable mate to himself, 'I'd risk it, and ask whether I might write to her.'

This chance of imperilling a promising career did not occur, however; the steamer slowly edged away from the schooner, and, picking her way between a tier of lighters, steamed slowly into clearer water.

'Full speed ahead!' roared the skipper down the tube.

The engineer responded, and the mate gazed in a melancholy fashion at the water as it rapidly widened between the two vessels. Then his face brightened up suddenly as the girl ran up on deck and waved her hand. Hardly able to believe his eyes, he waved back. The girl gesticulated violently, now pointing to the steamer, and then to the schooner.

'By George, that girl's taken a fancy to you,' said the skipper. 'She wants you to go back.'

The mate sighed. 'Seems like it,' he said modestly.

To his astonishment the girl was now joined by her menfolk, who also waved hearty farewells, and, throwing their arms about, shouted incoherently.

'Darned if they haven't all taken a fancy to you,' said the puzzled skipper; 'the old man's getting the speaking trumpet now. What does he say?'

'Something about life, I think,' said the mate.

'They're more like jumping-jacks than anything else,' said the skipper. 'Just look at them.'

The mate looked, and, as the distance, increased, sprang on to the side, and, his eyes dim with emotion, waved tender farewells. If it had not been for the presence of the skipper—a tremendous stickler for decorum—he would have kissed his hand.

It was not until Gravesend was passed, and the side-lights of the shipping were trying to show in the gathering dusk, that he awoke from his tender apathy. It is probable that it would have lasted longer than that but a sudden wail of anguish and terror which proceeded from the cabin and rang out on the still warm air.

'Sakes alive!' said the skipper, starting; 'what's that?'

Before the mate could reply, the companion was pushed back, and a middle-aged woman, labouring under strong excitement, appeared on deck.

'You villain!' she screamed excitably, rushing up to the mate. 'Take me back; take me back!'

'What's all this, Harry?' demanded the skipper sternly.

'He–he–he–asked me to go into the cabin–cabin,' sobbed Mrs Jansell, 'and sent me to sleep, and too–too–took me away. My husband'll kill me; I know he will. Take me back.'

'What do you want to be taken back to be killed for?' interposed one of the men judicially.

'I might have known what he meant when he said I brightened the cabin up,' said Mrs Jansell; 'and when he said he thought my daughter and I were sisters. He said he'd like me to sit there always, the wretch!'

'Did you say that?' inquired the skipper fiercely.

'Well, I did,' said the miserable mate; 'but I didn't mean her to take it that way. She went to sleep, and I forgot all about her.'

'What did you say such silly lies for, then?' demanded the skipper.

The mate hung his head.

'Old enough to be your mother too,' said the skipper severely. 'Here's a nice thing to happen aboard my ship.'

'Take me back,' wailed Mrs Jansell; 'you don't know how jealous my husband is.'

'He won't hurt you,' said the skipper kindly; 'he won't be jealous of a woman of your age; that is, not if he's got any sense. You'll have to go as far as Boston with us now. I've lost too much time already to go back.'

'You must take me back,' said Mrs Jansell passionately.

'I'm not going back for anybody,' said the skipper. 'But you can make your mind quite easy; you're as safe aboard my ship as you would be alone on a raft in the middle of the Atlantic; and as for the mate, he was only chaffing you. Weren't you, Harry?'

The mate made some reply, but neither Mrs Jansell, the skipper, nor the men, who were all listening eagerly, caught it, and his unfortunate victim, accepting the inevitable, walked to the side of the ship and gazed disconsolately astern.

It was not until the following morning that the mate, who had received orders to mess for'ard, saw her, and ignoring the fact that everybody suspended work to listen, walked up and bade her good morning.

'Harry,' said the skipper warningly.

'All right,' said the mate shortly. 'I want to speak to you very particularly,' he said nervously, and led his listener aft, followed by three of the crew who came to clean the brass-work, and who listened mutinously when they were ordered to defer unwonted industry to a more fitting time. The deck clear, the mate began, and in a long rambling statement, which Mrs Jansell at first thought the ravings of lunacy, acquainted her with the real state of his feelings.

'I never did!' said she, when he had finished. 'Never! Why, you hadn't seen her before yesterday.'

'Of course I shall take you back by train,' said the mate, 'and tell your husband how sorry I am.'

'I might have suspected something when you said all those nice things to me,' said the mollified lady. 'Well, you must take your chance, like all the rest of them. She can only say

"No", again. It'll explain this affair better, that's one thing; but I expect they'll laugh at you.'

'I don't care,' said the mate stoutly. 'You're on my side, aren't you?'

Mrs Jansell laughed, and the mate, having succeeded beyond his hopes in the establishment of amicable relations, went about his duties with a light heart.

By the time they reached Boston the morning was far advanced, and after the *Gem* was comfortably berthed he obtained permission from the skipper to accompany the fair passenger to London, beguiling the long railway journey by every means in his power. Despite his efforts, however, the journey began to pall upon his companion, and it was not until evening was well advanced that they found themselves in the narrow streets of Limehouse.

'We'll see how the land lies first,' said he, as they approached the wharf and made their way cautiously on to the quay.

The *Aquila* was still alongside, and the mate's heart thumped violently as he saw the cause of all the trouble sitting alone on the deck. She rose with a little start as her mother stepped carefully aboard, and, running to her, kissed her affectionately, and sat her down on the hatches.

'Poor mother,' she said caressingly. 'What did you bring that lunatic back with you for?'

'He would come,' said Mrs Jansell. 'Hush! here comes your father.'

The master of the *Aquila* came on deck as she spoke, and walking slowly up to the group, stood sternly regarding them. Under his gaze the mate breathlessly reeled off his tale, noticing with somewhat mixed feelings the widening grin of his listener as he proceeded.

'Well, you're a lively sort of man,' said the skipper as he finished. 'In one day you tie up your own ship, run off with my wife, and lose us a tide. Are you always like that?'

'I want somebody to look after me, I suppose,' said the mate, with a side glance at Nancy.

'Well, we'd put you up for the night,' said the skipper with his arm round his wife's shoulders; 'but you're such a chap. I'm afraid you'd burn the ship down, or something. What do you think, old girl?'

'I think we'll try him this once,' said his wife. 'And now I'll go down and see about supper. I want it.'

The old couple went below, and the young one remained on deck. Nancy went and leaned against the side; and as she appeared to have quite forgotten his presence, the mate, after some hesitation, joined her.

'Hadn't you better go down and get some supper?' she asked.

'I'd sooner stay here, if you don't mind,' said the mate. 'I like watching the lights going up and down; I could stay here for hours.'

'I'll leave you, then,' said the girl; 'I'm hungry.'

She tripped lightly off with a smothered laugh, leaving the fairly-trapped man gazing indignantly at the lights which had lured him to destruction.

From below he heard the cheerful clatter of crockery, accompanied by a savoury incense, and talk and laughter. He imagined the girl making fun of his sentimental reasons for staying on deck; but, too proud to meet her ironical glances, stayed doggedly where he was, resolving to be off by the first train in the morning. He was roused from his gloom by a slight touch on his arm, and, turning sharply, saw the girl by his side.

'Supper's quite ready,' said she soberly. 'And if you want to admire the lights very much, come up and see them when I do—after supper.'

An Elaborate Elopement

I HAVE always had a slight suspicion that the following narrative is not quite true. It was related to me by an old seaman who, among other incidents of a somewhat adventurous career, claimed to have received Napoleon's sword at the battle of Trafalgar, and a wound in the back at Waterloo. I prefer to tell it in my own way, his being so garnished with nautical terms and expletives as to be half unintelligible and somewhat horrifying. Our talk had been of love and courtship, and after making me a present of several tips, invented by himself, and considered invaluable by his friends, he related this story of the courtship of a chum of his as illustrating the great lengths to which young bloods were prepared to go in his days to attain their ends.

It was a fine clear day in June when Hezekiah Lewis, captain and part owner of the schooner *Thames*, bound from London to Aberdeen, anchored off the little out-of-the-way town of Orford in Suffolk. Among other antiquities, the town possessed Hezekiah's widowed mother, and when there was no very great hurry—the world went slower in those days—the dutiful son used to go ashore in the ship's boat, and after a filial tap at his mother's window, which often startled the old woman considerably, pass on his way to see a young lady to whom he had already proposed five times without effect.

The mate and crew of the schooner, seven all told, drew up in a little knot as the skipper, in his shore-going clothes, appeared on deck, and regarded him with an air of grinning, mysterious interest.

'Now you all know what you have got to do?' queried the skipper.

'Ay, ay,' replied the crew, grinning still more deeply.

Hezekiah regarded them closely, and then ordering the boat to be lowered, scrambled over the side, and was pulled swiftly towards the shore.

A sharp scream as he tapped at his mother's window, assured him that the old lady was alive and well, and he continued on his way until he brought up at a small but pretty house in the next road.

'Morning, Mr Rumbolt,' said he heartily to a stout, red-faced man, who sat smoking in the doorway.

'Morning, cap'n, morning,' said the red-faced man.

'Is the rheumatism any better?' inquired Hezekiah anxiously, as he grasped the other's huge hand.

'So, so,' said the other. 'But it isn't the rheumatism so much that troubles me,' he resumed, lowering his voice, and looking round cautiously. 'It's Kate.'

'What?' said the skipper.

'You've heard of a man being henpecked?' continued Mr Rumbolt, in tones of husky confidence.

The captain nodded.

'I'm *chick-pecked*,' murmured the other.

'What?' inquired the astonished mariner again.

'Chick-pecked,' repeated Mr Rumbolt firmly. 'CHICK-PECKED. D'you understand me?'

The captain said that he did, and stood silent awhile, with the air of a man who wants to say something, but is half afraid to. At last, with a desperate appearance of resolution, he bent down to the old man's ear.

'That's the deaf one,' said Mr Rumbolt promptly.

Hezekiah changed ears, speaking at first slowly and awkwardly, but becoming more fluent as he warmed with his subject; while the expression on his listener's face gradually changed from incredulous bewilderment to one of uncontrollable mirth. He became so uproarious that he had to push the captain away from him, and lean back in his chair and choke and laugh until he nearly lost his breath, at which crisis a remarkably pretty girl appeared from the back of the house, and patted him with hearty good will.

'That'll do, my dear,' said the choking Mr Rumbolt. 'Here's Captain Lewis.'

'I can see him,' said his daughter calmly. 'What's he standing on one leg for?'

The skipper, who really was standing in a somewhat constrained attitude, coloured violently, and planted both feet firmly on the ground.

'As I was passing close by, Miss Rumbolt,' said he, 'and coming ashore to see mother——'

To the captain's discomfort, manifestations of a further attack on the part of Mr Rumbolt appeared, but were promptly quelled by the daughter.

'Mother?' she repeated encouragingly.

'I thought I'd come on and ask you just to pay a sort of flying visit to the *Thames*.'

'Thank you, I'm comfortable enough where I am,' said the girl.

'I've got a couple of monkeys and a bear aboard, which I'm taking to a menagerie in Aberdeen,' continued the captain, 'and the thought struck me you might possibly like to see them.'

'Well, I don't know,' said the damsel in a flutter. 'Is it a big bear?'

'Have you ever seen an elephant?' inquired Hezekiah cautiously.

'Only in pictures,' replied the girl.

'Well, it's as big as that, nearly,' said he.

The temptation was irresistible, and Miss Rumbolt, telling her father she would not be long, disappeared into the house in search of her hat and jacket, and ten minutes later the brawny rowers were gazing their fill into her deep blue eyes as she sat in the stern of the boat, and told Lewis to behave himself.

It was only a short pull out to the schooner, and Miss Rumbolt was soon on deck, lavishing endearments on the monkey, and energetically prodding the bear with a handspike to make him growl. The noise of the offended animal as he strove to get through the bars of his cage was terrific, and the girl was in full enjoyment of it, when she became aware of a louder noise still, and, turning round, saw the seamen at the windlass.

'Why, what are they doing?' she demanded, 'getting up anchor?'

'Ahoy, there!' shouted Hezekiah sternly. 'What are you doing with that windlass?'

As he spoke, the anchor peeped over the edge of the bows, and one of the seamen running past them took the helm.

'Now then,' shouted the fellow, 'stand by. Look lively there with those sails.'

Obeying a light touch of the helm, the schooner's bowsprit slowly swung round from the land, and the crew, hauling lustily on the ropes, began to hoist the sails.'

'What the devil are you up to?' thundered the skipper. Have you all gone mad? What does it all mean?'

'It means,' said one of the seamen, whose fat, amiable face was marred by a fearful scowl, 'that we've got a new skipper.'

'Good heavens, a mutiny!' exclaimed the skipper, starting melodramatically against the cage, and starting hastily away again. 'Where's the mate?'

'He's with us,' said another seaman, brandishing his sheath knife, and scowling fearfully. 'He's our new captain.'

In confirmation of this the mate now appeared from below with an axe in his hand, and, approaching his captain, roughly ordered him below.

'I'll defend this lady with my life,' cried Hezekiah, taking the handspike from Kate, and raising it above his head.

'Nobody'll hurt a hair of her beautiful head,' said the mate, with a tender smile.

'Then I yield,' said the skipper, drawing himself up, and delivering the handspike with the air of a defeated admiral tendering his sword.

'Good,' said the mate briefly, as one of the men took it.

'What!' demanded Miss Rumbolt excitedly, 'aren't you going to fight them? Here, give me the handspike.'

Before the mate could interfere, the sailor, with thoughtless obedience, handed it over, and Miss Rumbolt at once tried to knock him over the head. Being thwarted in this design by the man taking flight, she lost her temper entirely, and bore down like a hurricane on the remaining members of the crew who were just approaching.

They scattered at once, and ran up the rigging like cats, and for a few moments the girl held the deck; then the mate crept up behind her, and with the air of a man whose job exactly suited him, clasped her tightly round the waist, while one of the seamen disarmed her.

'You must both go below till we've settled what to do with you,' said the mate, reluctantly releasing her.

With a wistful glance at the handspike, the girl walked to the cabin, followed slowly by the skipper.

'This is a bad business,' said the latter, shaking his head solemnly, as the indignant Miss Rumbolt seated herself.

'Don't talk to me, you coward!' said the girl energetically.

The skipper started.

'*I* made three of them run,' said Miss Rumbolt, 'and you did nothing. You just stood still, and let them take the ship. I'm ashamed of you.'

118

The skipper's defence was interrupted by a hoarse voice shouting to them to come on deck, where they found the mutinous crew gathered aft round the mate. The girl cast a look at the shore, which was now dim and indistinct, and turned somewhat pale as the serious nature of her position forced itself upon her.

'Lewis,' said the mate.

'Well,' growled the skipper.

'This ship's going into the lace and brandy trade, and if you're sensible you can go with it as mate, d'you hear?'

'And suppose I do; what about the lady?' inquired the captain.

'You and the lady'll have to get spliced,' said the mate sternly. 'Then there'll be no tales told. A Scotch marriage is as good as any, and we'll just lay off and put you ashore and you can get tied up as right as ninepence.'

'Marry a coward like that?' demanded Miss Rumbolt, with spirit; 'not if I know it. Why, I'd sooner marry that old man at the helm.'

'Old Bill's married already to my certain knowledge,' spoke up one of the sailors. 'The lady's got to marry Cap'n Lewis, so don't let's have any fuss about it.'

'I won't,' said the lady, stamping violently.

The mutineers appeared to be in a dilemma, and, following the example of the mate, scratched their heads thoughtfully.

'We thought you liked him,' said the mate, at last, feebly.

'You had no business to think,' said Miss Rumbolt. 'You are bad men, and you'll all be punished, every one of you; I shall come and see it.'

'The cap'n's welcome to her for me,' murmured the helmsman in a husky whisper to the man next to him. 'The vixen!'

'Very good,' said the mate. 'If you won't, you won't. This end of the ship'll belong to you after eight o'clock at night. Lewis, you must go for'ard with the men.'

'And what are you going to do with me after?' inquired the fair prisoner.

The seven men shrugged their shoulders helplessly, and Hezekiah lounged moodily about, a prisoner at large. At eight o'clock Miss Rumbolt was given the key of the state-room, and the men who were not in the watch went below.

The morning broke fine and clear with a light breeze, which, towards midday, dropped entirely, and the schooner lay rocking lazily on a sea of glassy smoothness. The sun beat fiercely down, bringing the fresh paint on the taffrail up in blisters, and sorely trying the tempers of the men who were doing odd jobs on deck.

The cabin, where the two victims of a mutinous crew had retired for coolness, got more and more stuffy, until at length even the scorching deck seemed preferable, and the girl, with a faint hope of finding a shady corner, went languidly up the companion-ladder.

For some time the skipper sat alone, pondering gloomily over the state of affairs as he smoked his short pipe. He was aroused at length from his apathy by the sound of the companion being noisily closed, while loud frightened cries and hurrying footsteps on deck announced that something extraordinary was happening. As he rose to his feet he was confronted by Kate Rumbolt, who, panting and excited, waved a big key before him.

'I've done it,' she cried, her eyes sparkling.

'Done what?' shouted the mystified skipper.

'Let the bear loose,' said the girl. 'Ha, ha! you should have seen them run. You should have seen the fat sailor!'

'Let the—phew—let the—— Good heavens! here's a pretty kettle of fish!' he choked.

'Listen to them shouting,' cried the exultant Kate, clapping her hands. 'Just listen.'

'Those shouts are from aloft,' said Hezekiah sternly, 'where you and I ought to be.'

'I've closed the companion,' said the girl reassuringly.

'Closed the companion!' repeated Hezekiah, as he drew his knife. 'He can smash it like cardboard, if the fit takes him. Go in here.'

He opened the door of his state-room.

'Shan't!' said Miss Rumbolt politely.

'Go in at once!' cried the skipper. 'Quick with you.'

'Sha—' began Miss Rumbolt again. Then she caught his eye, and went in like a lamb. 'You come too,' she said prettily.

'I've got to look after my ship and my men,' said the skipper. 'I suppose you thought the ship would steer itself, didn't you?'

'Mutineers deserve to be eaten,' whimpered Miss Rumbolt piously, somewhat taken aback by the skipper's demeanour.

Hezekiah looked at her.

'They're not mutineers, Kate,' he said quietly. 'It was just a piece of mad folly of mine. They're as honest a set of old sea dogs as ever breathed, and I only hope they are all safe up aloft. I'm going to lock you in; but don't be frightened, it shan't hurt you.'

He slammed the door on her protests, and locked it, and, slipping the key of the cage in his pocket, took a firm grip of his knife, and, running up the steps, gained the deck. Then his breath came more freely, for the mate, who was standing a little way up the fore rigging, after tempting the bear with his foot, had succeeded in dropping a noose over its head. The brute made a furious attempt to extricate itself, but the men hurried down with other lines, and in a short space of time the bear presented much the same appearance as the lion in *Aesop's Fables*, and was dragged and pushed, a heated and indignant mass of fur, back to its cage.

Having locked up one prisoner the skipper went below and released the other, who passed quickly from a somewhat hysterical condition to one of such haughty disdain that the captain was thoroughly cowed, and stood humbly aside to let her pass.

The fat seaman was standing in front of the cage as she reached it, and regarding the bear with much satisfaction until Kate sidled up to him, and begged him, as a personal favour to go in the cage and undo it.

'Undo it! Why he'd kill me!' gasped the fat seaman, aghast at such simplicity.

'I don't think he would,' said his tormentor, with a bewitching smile; 'and I'll wear a lock of your hair all my life if you do. But you'd better give it to me before you go in.'

'I'm not going in,' said the fat sailor shortly.

'Not for me?' queried Kate archly.

'Not for fifty like you,' replied the old man firmly. 'He nearly had me when he was loose. I can't think how he got out.'

'Why, I let him out,' said Miss Rumbolt airily. 'Just for a little run. How would you like to be shut up all day?'

The sailor was just going to tell her with more fluency than politeness when he was interrupted.

'That'll do,' said the skipper, who had come behind them. 'Go for'ard you. There's been enough of this fooling; the lady thought you had taken the ship. Thompson, I'll take the helm; there's a little wind coming. Stand by there.'

He walked aft and relieved the steersman, awkwardly conscious that the men were becoming more and more interested in the situation, and also that Kate could hear some of their remarks. As he pondered over the subject, and tried to think of a way out of it, the cause of all the trouble came and stood by him.

'Did my father know of this?' she inquired.

'I don't know that he did exactly,' said the skipper uneasily. 'I just told him not to expect you back that night.'

'And what did he say?' said she.

'Said he wouldn't sit up,' said the skipper, grinning despite himself.

Kate drew a breath the length of which boded no good to her parent, and looked over the side.

'I was afraid of that traveller chap from Ipswich,' said Hezekiah, after a pause. 'Your father told me he was hanging round you again, so I thought I—well, I was a stupid fool anyway.'

'See how ridiculous you have made me look before all these men,' said the girl angrily.

'They've been with me for years,' said Hezekiah apologetically, 'and the mate said it was a magnificent idea. He quite raved about it. I wouldn't have done it with some crews, but we've had some dirty times together, and they've stood by me well. But of course that's nothing to do with you. It's been an adventure I'm very sorry for, very.'

'A pretty safe adventure for *you*,' said the girl scornfully. '*You* didn't risk much. Look here, I like brave men. If you go in the cage and undo that bear, I'll marry you. That's what *I* call an adventure.'

'Smith,' called the skipper quietly, 'come and take the helm a bit.'

The seaman obeyed, and Lewis, accompanied by the girl, walked forward.

At the bear's cage he stopped, and, fumbling in his pocket for the key, steadily regarded the brute as it lay gnashing its teeth, and trying in vain to bite the ropes which bound it.

'You're afraid,' said the girl tauntingly; 'you're quite white.'

The captain made no reply, but eyed her so steadily that her gaze fell. He drew the key from his pocket and inserted it in the huge lock, and was just turning it, when a soft arm was drawn through his, and a soft voice murmured sweetly in his ear, 'Never mind about the old bear.'

And he did not mind.

The Cook of the *Gannet*

'ALL ready for sea, and no cook,' said the mate of the schooner *Gannet*, gloomily. 'What's become of all the cooks I can't think.'

'They most of them ship as mates now,' said the skipper, grinning. 'But you needn't worry about that; I've got one coming aboard tonight. I'm trying a new experiment, George.'

'I knew a chemist who tried one,' said George, 'and it blew him out of the window; but I never heard of shipmasters trying them.'

'There's all kinds of experiments,' rejoined the other. 'What do you say to a lady cook, George?'

'A *what*?' asked the mate in tones of strong amazement. 'What, aboard a schooner?'

'Why not?' inquired the skipper warmly; 'why not? There's plenty of them ashore—why not aboard ship?'

''T'isn't proper, for one thing,' said the mate virtuously.

'I shouldn't have expected you to have thought of that,' said the other unkindly. 'Besides, they have stewardesses on big ships, and what's the difference? She's a sort of relation of mine, too—cousin of my wife's, a widow woman, and a good sensible age, and as the doctor told her to take a sea voyage for the benefit of her health, she's coming with me for six months as cook. She'll take her meals with us; but, of course, the men are not to know the relationship.'

'What about sleeping accommodation?' inquired the mate, with the air of a man putting a poser.

'I've thought of that,' replied the other; 'it's all arranged.'

The mate with an uncompromising air, waited for information.

'She—she's to have your berth, George,' continued the skipper, without looking at him. 'You can have that nice, large, airy locker.'

'The one the biscuits and onions are kept in?' inquired George.

The skipper nodded.

'I think, if it's all the same to you,' said the mate, with laboured politeness, 'I'll wait until the butter keg's empty, and crowd into that.'

'It's no use your making yourself unpleasant about it,' said the skipper, 'not a bit. The arrangements are made now, and here she comes.'

Following his gaze, the mate looked up as a stout, comely-looking woman of middle age came along the jetty, followed by the watchman staggering under a box of enormous proportions.

'Jim!' cried the lady.

'Halloa!' cried the skipper, starting uneasily at the title. We've been expecting you for some time.'

'There's a row on with the cabman,' said the lady calmly. 'This silly old man'—the watchman snorted fiercely—'let the box go through the window getting it off the top, the cabman wants *me* to pay. He's out there using language, and he keeps calling me grandma—I want you to have him locked up.'

'Come down below now,' said the skipper; 'we'll see about the cab. Mrs Blossom—my mate. George, go and send that cab away.'

Mrs Blossom, briefly acknowledging the introduction, followed the skipper to the cabin, while the mate, growling under his breath, went out to enter into a verbal contest in which he was from the first hopelessly overmatched.

The new cook, being somewhat fatigued with her journey, withdrew at an early hour, and the sun was well up when she appeared on deck next morning. The wharves and warehouses of the night before had disappeared, and the schooner, under a fine spread of canvas, was just passing Tilbury.

'There's one thing I must put a stop to,' said the skipper, as he and the mate, after an admirably-cooked breakfast, stood together talking. 'The men seem to be hanging round that galley too much.'

'What can you expect?' demanded the mate. 'They've all got their Sunday clothes on too, pretty dears.'

'Hi, you Bill!' cried the skipper. 'What are you doing there?'

'Lending cook a hand with the saucepans, sir,' said Bill, an oakum-bearded man of sixty.

'There isn't any call for him to come here at all, sir,' shouted another seaman, putting his head out of the galley. 'Cook and I are lifting them very well.'

'Come out, both of you, or I'll start you with a rope!' roared the irritated commander.

'What's the matter?' inquired Mrs Blossom. 'They're not doing any harm.'

'I can't have them there,' said the skipper gruffly. 'They've got other things to do.'

'I must have some assistance with that boiler and the saucepans,' said Mrs Blossom decidedly, 'so don't you interfere with what doesn't concern you, Jimmy.'

'That's mutiny,' whispered the horrified mate. 'Sheer, rank mutiny.'

'She doesn't know any better,' whispered the other back. 'Cook, you mustn't talk like that to the cap'n—what the mate

126

and I tell you to do you must do. You don't understand yet, but it'll come easier by and by.'

'*Will* it,' demanded Mrs Blossom loudly; '*will* it? I don't think it will. How dare you talk to me like that, Jim Harris? You ought to be ashamed of yourself!'

'My name's Cap'n Harris,' said the skipper stiffly.

'Well, *Captain* Harris,' said Mrs Blossom scornfully; 'and what'll happen if I don't do as you and that other shamefaced looking man tell me?'

'We hope it won't come to that,' said Harris, with quiet dignity, as he paused at the companion. 'But the mate's in charge just now, and I warn you he's a very severe man. Don't stand any nonsense, George.'

With these brave words the skipper disappeared below, and the mate, after one glance at the dauntless and imposing attitude of Mrs Blossom, walked to the side and became engrossed in a passing steamer. A hum of wondering admiration arose from the crew, and the cook, thoroughly satisfied with her victory, returned to the scene of her labours.

For the next twenty-four hours Mrs Blossom reigned supreme, and performed the cooking for the vessel, assisted by five ministering seamen. The weather was fine, and the wind light, and the two officers were at their wits' end to find jobs for the men.

'Why don't you put your foot down,' grumbled the mate, as a burst of happy laughter came from the direction of the galley. 'The idea of men laughing like that aboard ship; they're carrying on just as though we weren't here.'

'Will you stand by me?' demanded the skipper, pale but determined.

'Of course I will,' said the other indignantly.

'Now, my lads,' said Harris, stepping forward, 'I can't have you chaps hanging round the galley all day; you're getting in cook's way and hindering her. Just get your knives out; I'll have the masts scraped.'

'You just stay where you are,' said Mrs Blossom. 'When they're in my way, I'll soon let them know.'

'Did you hear what I said?' thundered the skipper, as the men hesitated.

'Aye, aye, sir,' muttered the crew, moving off.

'How dare you interfere with me?' said Mrs Blossom hotly, as she realized defeat. 'Ever since I've been on this ship you've been trying to aggravate me. I wonder the men don't hit you, you nasty, ginger-whiskered little man.'

'Go on with your work,' said the skipper, fondly stroking the maligned whiskers.

'Don't you talk to me, Jim Harris,' said Mrs Blossom, quivering with wrath. 'Don't you give *me* any of your airs. *Who borrowed five pounds from my poor dead husband just before he died, and never paid it back?*'

'Go on with your work,' repeated the skipper, with pale lips.

'*Whose Uncle Benjamin had three weeks?*' demanded Mrs Blossom darkly. '*Whose Uncle Joseph had to go abroad without stopping to pack up?*'

The skipper made no reply, but the anxiety of the crew to have these vital problems solved was so manifest that he turned his back on the virago and went towards the mate, who at that moment dipped hurriedly to escape a wet dish-clout. The two men regarded each other, pale with anxiety.

'Now, you just move off,' said Mrs Blossom, shaking another clout at them. 'I won't have you hanging about my galley. Keep to your own end of the ship.'

The skipper drew himself up haughtily, but the effect was somewhat marred by one eye, which dwelt persistently on the clout, and after a short inward struggle he moved off, accompanied by the mate. Wellington himself would have been nonplussed by a wet cloth in the hands of a fearless woman.

'She'll just have to have her own way till we get to Llanelly,' said the indignant skipper, 'and then I'll send her home by train and ship another cook. I knew she'd got a temper, but I didn't know it was like this. She's the last woman that sets foot on my ship—that's all she's done for her sex.'

In happy ignorance of her impending doom Mrs Blossom went blithely about her duties, assisted by a crew whose admiration for her increased by leaps and bounds; and the only thing which ventured to interfere with her was a stiff Atlantic roll, which they encountered upon round the Land's End.

The first intimation Mrs Blossom had of it was the falling of small utensils in the galley. After she had picked them up and replaced them several times, she went out to investigate, and discovered that the schooner was dipping her bows to big green waves, and rolling with much straining and creaking from side to side. A fine spray, which broke over the bows and flew over the vessel, drove her back into the galley, which had suddenly developed an unaccountable stuffiness; but, though the crew to a man advised her to lie down and have a cup of tea, she repelled them with scorn, and with pale face and compressed lips stuck to her post.

Two days later they made fast to the quay at Llanelly, and half an hour later the skipper called the mate down to the cabin, and, handing him some money, told him to pay the cook off and ship another. The mate declined.

'You obey orders,' said the skipper fiercely, 'else you and I will quarrel.'

'I've got a wife and family,' urged the mate.

'Pooh!' said the skipper. 'Rubbish!'

'And uncles,' added the mate rebelliously.

'Very good,' said the skipper, glaring. 'We'll ship the other cook first and let him settle it. After all, I don't see why we should fight his battles for him.'

The mate, being agreeable, went off at once; and when Mrs Blossom, after a little shopping ashore, returned to the *Gannet* she found the galley in the possession of one of the fattest cooks that ever broke ship's biscuit.

'Hullo!' said she, realizing the situation at a glance, 'what are you doing here?'

'Cooking,' said the other gruffly. Then, catching sight of his questioner, he smiled amorously and winked at her.

'Don't you wink at me,' said Mrs Blossom wrathfully. 'Come out of that galley.'

'There's room for both,' said the new cook persuasively. 'Come in and put your head on my shoulder.'

Utterly unprepared for this mode of attack, Mrs Blossom lost her nerve, and, instead of storming the galley, as she had fully intended, drew back and retired to the cabin, where she found a short note from the skipper, enclosing her pay, and requesting her to take the train home. After reading this she went ashore again, returning presently with a big bundle, which she placed on the cabin table in front of Harris and the mate, who had just begun tea.

'I'm not going home by train,' said she, opening the bundle, which contained a spirit kettle and provisions. 'I'm going back with you; but I'm not going to be beholden to you for anything—I'm going to board myself.'

After this declaration she made herself tea and sat down. The meal proceeded in silence, though occasionally she astonished her companions by little mysterious laughs, which caused them slight uneasiness. As she made no hostile demonstration, however, they became reassured, and congratulated themselves upon the success of their manœuvre.

'How long shall we be getting back to London, do you think?' inquired Mrs Blossom at last.

'We shall probably sail Tuesday night, and it may be anything from six days upwards,' answered the skipper. 'If this wind holds it will probably be upwards.'

To his great concern Mrs Blossom put her handkerchief over her face, and, shaking with suppressed laughter, rose from the table and left the cabin.

The couple left eyeing each other wonderingly.

'Did I say anything particularly funny, George?' inquired the skipper, after some deliberation.

'Didn't strike me so,' said the mate carelessly; 'I expect she's thought of something else to say about your family. She wouldn't be as good-tempered as all that for nothing. I feel curious to know what it is.'

'If you paid more attention to your own business,' said the skipper, his choler rising, 'you'd get on better. A mate who was a good seaman wouldn't have let a cook go on like this—it's not discipline.'

He went off in dudgeon, and a coolness sprang up between them, which lasted until the bustle of starting in the small hours of Wednesday morning.

Once under way the day passed uneventfully, the schooner crawling sluggishly down the coast of Wales, and, when the skipper turned in that night, it was with the pleasant conviction that Mrs Blossom had shot her last bolt, and, like a sensible woman, was going to accept her defeat. From this pleasing idea he was aroused suddenly by the watch stamping heavily on the deck overhead.

'What's up?' cried the skipper, darting up the companion-ladder.

'I don't know,' said Bill, who was at the wheel, shakily. 'Mrs Blossom came up on deck a little while ago, and since then there's been three or four heavy splashes.'

'She can't have gone overboard,' said the skipper, in tones to which he manfully strove to impart a semblance of anxiety.

'No, here she is. Anything wrong, Mrs Blossom?'

'Not as far as I'm concerned,' replied the lady, passing him and going below.

'You've been dreaming, Bill,' said the skipper sharply.

'I haven't,' said Bill stoutly. 'I tell you I heard splashes. It's my belief she coaxed the cook up on deck, and then pushed him overboard. A woman could do anything with a man like that cook.'

'I'll soon see,' said the mate, and walking forward he put his head down the fore-scuttle and yelled for the cook.

'Aye, aye, sir,' answered a voice sleepily, while the other men started up in their bunks. 'Do you want me?'

'Bill thinks somebody has gone overboard,' said the mate. 'Are you all here?'

In answer to this the mystified men turned out all standing, and came on deck yawning and rubbing their eyes, while the mate explained the situation. Before he had finished the cook suddenly darted off to the galley, and the next moment the forlorn cry of a bereaved soul broke on their startled ears.

'What is it?' cried the mate.

'Come here!' shouted the cook, 'look at this!'

He struck a match and held it aloft in his shaking fingers, and the men, who were worked up to a great pitch of excitement and expected to see something ghastly, after staring hard for some time in vain, profanely requested him to be more explicit.

'She's thrown all the saucepans and things overboard,' said the cook with desperate calmness. 'This lid of a tea-kettle is all that's left for me to do the cooking in.'

The *Gannet*, manned by seven famine-stricken misogynists, reached London six days later, the skipper obstinately refusing to put in at an intermediate port to replenish his stock of hardware. The most he would consent to do was to try and borrow from a passing vessel, but the unseemly behaviour of the master of a brig, who lost two hours owing to their efforts to obtain a saucepan from him, utterly discouraged any further attempts in that direction, and they settled down to a diet of biscuits and water, and salt beef scorched on the stove.

Mrs Blossom, unwilling perhaps to witness their sufferings, remained below, and when they reached London, only consented to land under the supervision of a guard of honour, composed of all the able-bodied men on the wharf.

A Benefit Performance

IN the small front parlour of No. 3, Mermaid Passage, Sunset Bay, Jackson Pepper, ex-pilot, sat in a state of indignant collapse, tenderly feeling a cheek on which the print of hasty fingers still lingered.

The room, which was in excellent order, showed no signs of the tornado which had passed through it, and Jackson Pepper, looking vaguely round, was dimly reminded of those tropical hurricanes he had read about which would strike only the objects in their path, and leave all other undisturbed.

In this instance he had been the object, and the tornado, after obliterating him, had passed up the small staircase which led from the room, leaving him listening anxiously to its distant mutterings.

To his great discomfort the storm showed signs of coming up again, and he had barely time to effect an appearance of easy unconcern, which accorded ill with the flush afore-mentioned, when a big, red-faced woman came heavily downstairs and burst into the room.

'You have made me ill again,' she said severely, 'and now I hope you are satisfied with your work. You'll kill me before you have done with me!'

The ex-pilot shifted on his chair.

'You're not fit to have a wife,' continued Mrs Pepper,

'aggravating them and upsetting them! Any other woman would have left you long ago!'

'We've only been married three months,' Pepper reminded her.

'Don't talk to me!' said his wife; 'it seems more like a lifetime!'

'It seems a long time to *me*,' said the ex-pilot, plucking up a little courage.

'That's right!' said his wife, striding over to where he sat. 'Say you're tired of me; say you wish you hadn't married me! You coward! Ah! if my poor first husband was only alive and sitting in that chair now instead of you, how happy I would be!'

'If he likes to come and take it he's welcome!' said Pepper; 'it's my chair, and it was my father's before me, but there's no man living I would sooner give it to than your first. Ah! he knew what he was about when the *Dolphin* went down, he did. I don't blame him, though.'

'What do you mean?' demanded his wife.

'It's my belief that he didn't go down with her,' said Pepper, crossing over to the staircase and standing with his hand on the door.

'Didn't go down with her?' repeated his wife scornfully. 'What became of him then? Where's he been for the last thirty years?'

'In hiding!' said Pepper spitefully, and passed hastily upstairs.

The room above was charged with memories of the late lamented. His portrait in oils hung above the mantelpiece, smaller portraits—specimens of the photographer's want of art—were scattered about the room, while various personal effects, including a mammoth pair of sea-boots, stood in a corner. On all these articles the eye of Jackson Pepper dwelt with an air of chastened regret.

'It would be a rum go if he did turn up after all,' he said to

135

himself softly, as he sat on the edge of the bed. 'I've heard of such things in books. I daresay she'd be disappointed if she did see him now. Thirty years makes a bit of difference in a man.'

'Jackson!' cried his wife from below, 'I'm going out. If you want any dinner you can get it; if not, you can go without it!'

The front door slammed violently, and Jackson, advancing cautiously to the window, saw the form of his wife sailing majestically up the passage. Then he sat down again and resumed his meditations.

'If it wasn't for leaving all my property, I'd go,' he said gloomily. 'There's not a bit of comfort in the place! Nag, nag, nag, from morn till night! Ah, Cap'n Budd, you let me in for a nice thing when you went down with that boat of yours. Come back and fill those boots again; they're too big for me.'

He rose suddenly and stood gaping in the centre of the room, as a mad, hazy idea began to form in his brain. His eyes blinked and his face grew white with excitement. He pushed open the little lattice window, and sat looking abstractedly up the passage on to the bay beyond. Then he put on his hat, and, deep in thought, went out.

He was still thinking deeply as he boarded the train for London next morning, and watched Sunset Bay from the window until it disappeared round the curve. So many and various were the changes that flitted over his face that an old lady, whose seat he had taken, gave up her intention of apprising him of the fact, and indulged instead in a bitter conversation with her daughter, of which the erring Pepper was the unconscious object.

In the same preoccupied fashion he got on a Bayswater omnibus, and waited patiently for it to reach Poplar. Strange changes in the landscape, not to be accounted for by the mere lapse of time, led to explanations, and the conductor—a humane man—personally laid down the lines of his tour. Two hours later he stood in front of a small house painted in many colours, and, ringing the bell, inquired for Cap'n Crippen.

In response to his inquiry, a big man, with light blue eyes and a long grey beard, appeared, and, recognizing his visitor with a grunt of surprise, drew him heartily into the passage and thrust him into the parlour. He then shook hands with him, and, clapping him on the back, bawled lustily for the small boy who had opened the door.

'Pot of stout, bottle of gin, and two long pipes,' said he, as the boy came to the door and eyed the ex-pilot curiously.

At all these honest preparations for his welcome the heart of Jackson grew faint within him.

'Well, I call it good of you to come all this way to see me,' said the captain, after the boy had disappeared; 'but you always were warm-hearted, Pepper. And how's the wife?'

'Shocking!' said Pepper, with a groan.

'Ill?' inquired the captain.

'Ill-tempered,' said Pepper. 'In fact, cap'n, I don't mind telling you, she's killing me—slowly killing me!'

'Pooh!' said Crippen. 'Nonsense! You don't know how to manage her!'

'I thought perhaps you could advise me,' said the artful Pepper. 'I said to myself yesterday, "Pepper, go and see Cap'n Crippen. What he doesn't know about women and their management isn't worth knowing! If there's anyone who can get you out of a hole, it's him. He's got the power, and, what's more, he's got the will!"'

'What causes the temper?' inquired the captain, with his most judicial air, as he took the liquor from his messenger and carefully filled a couple of glasses.

'It's natural!' said his friend ruefully. 'She calls it having a high spirit herself. And she's so generous! She's got a married niece living in the place, and when that girl comes round and admires things—my things—she gives them to her! She gave her a sofa the other day, and, what's more, she made me help the girl carry it home!'

'Have you tried being sarcastic?' inquired the captain thoughtfully.

'I have,' said Pepper, with a shiver. 'The other day I said, very nastily, "Is there anything else you'd like my dear?" but she didn't understand it.'

'No?' said the captain.

'No,' said Pepper. 'She said I was very kind, and she'd like the clock; and what's more, she had it too! Red-haired hussy!'

The captain poured out some gin and drank it slowly. It was evident he was thinking deeply, and that he was much affected by his friend's troubles.

'There is only one way for me to get clear,' said Pepper, as he finished a thrilling recital of his wrongs, 'and that is, to find Cap'n Budd, her first husband.'

'Why, he's dead!' said Crippen, staring hard. 'Don't you waste your time looking for him!'

'I'm not going to,' said Pepper; 'but here's his portrait. He was a big man like you; he had blue eyes and a straight handsome nose, like you. If he'd lived to now he'd be almost your age, and very likely more like you than ever. He was a sailor; you've been a sailor.'

The captain stared at him in bewilderment.

'He had a wonderful way with women,' pursued Jackson hastily; 'you've got a wonderful way with women. More than that, you've got the most wonderful gift for acting I've ever seen. Ever since the time when you acted in that barn at Bristol I've never seen any actor I can honestly say I've liked—never! Look how you can imitate cats—better than Henry Irving himself!'

'I never had much chance, being at sea all my life,' said Crippen modestly.

'You've got the gift,' said Pepper impressively. 'It was born in you, and you'll never stop acting till the day of your death. You couldn't if you tried—you know you couldn't!'

The captain smiled deprecatingly.

'Now, I want you to do a performance for my benefit,' continued Pepper. 'I want you to act Cap'n Budd, who was lost in the *Dolphin* thirty years ago. There's only one man in England I'd trust with the part, and that's you.'

'Act Cap'n Budd!' gasped the astonished Crippen, putting down his glass and staring at his friend.

'The part is written here,' said the ex-pilot, producing a notebook from his breast pocket and holding it out to his friend. 'I've been keeping a log day by day of all the things she said about him, in the hopes of catching her out, but I never did. There's notes of his family, his ships, and a lot of silly things he used to say, which she thinks funny.'

'I couldn't do it!' said the captain seriously, as he took the book.

'You could do it if you liked,' said Pepper. 'Besides, think what a spree it'll be for you. Learn it by heart, then come down and claim her. Her name's Martha.'

'What good would it do you if I did?' inquired the captain, 'She'd soon find out!'

'You come down to Sunset Bay,' said Pepper, emphasizing his remarks with his forefinger; 'you claim your wife; you allude carefully to the things set down in this book; I give Martha back to you and bless you both. Then——'

'Then what?' inquired Crippen anxiously.

'You disappear!' concluded Pepper triumphantly; 'and, of course, believing her first husband is alive, she has to leave me. She's a very particular woman; and, besides that, I'd take care to let the neighbours know. I'm happy, you're happy, and, if she's not happy, why, she doesn't deserve to be.'

'I'll think it over,' said Crippen, 'and write and let you know.'

'Make up your mind now,' urged Pepper, reaching over and patting him encouragingly upon the shoulder. 'If you promise to do it, the thing's as good as done. I can see you now, coming in at that door and surprising her. Talk about acting!'

'Is she what you'd call a good-looking woman?' inquired Crippen.

'Very handsome!' said Pepper, looking out of the window.

'I couldn't do it!' said the captain. 'It wouldn't be right and fair to her.'

'I don't see that!' said Pepper. 'I never ought to have married her without being certain her first husband was dead. It isn't right, Crippen; say what you like, it isn't right!'

'If you put it that way,' said the captain hesitatingly.

'Have some more gin,' said the artful ex-pilot.

The captain had some more, and, what with flattery and gin, combined with the pleadings of his friend, began to consider the affair more favourably. Pepper stuck to his guns, and used them so well that when the captain saw him off that evening he was pledged up to the hilt to come down to Sunset Bay and impersonate the late Captain Budd on the following Thursday.

The ex-pilot passed the intervening days in a sort of trance, from which he only emerged to take nourishment, or answer the scoldings of his wife. On the eventful Thursday, however, his mood changed, and he went about in such a state of suppressed excitement that he could scarcely keep still.

'Bless me!' snapped Mrs Pepper, as he slowly perambulated the parlour that afternoon. 'What ails the man? Can't you keep still for five minutes?'

The ex-pilot stopped and eyed her solemnly, but before he could reply, his heart gave a great bound, for, from behind the geraniums which filled the window, he saw the face of Captain Crippen slowly rise and peer cautiously into the room. Before his wife could follow the direction of her husband's eyes it had disappeared.

'Somebody looking in at the window,' said Pepper, with forced calmness, in reply to his wife's eyebrows.

'Like their impudence!' said the unconscious woman, resuming her knitting, while her husband waited in vain for the captain to enter.

He waited some time, and then, half dead with excitement, sat down, and with shaking fingers lit his pipe. As he looked up the stalwart figure of the captain passed the window. During the next twenty minutes it passed seven times, and Pepper, coming to the not unnatural conclusion that his friend intended to pass the afternoon in the same unprofitable fashion, resolved to force his hand.

'Must be a tramp,' he said aloud.

'Who?' inquired his wife.

'Man keeps looking in at the window,' said Pepper desperately. 'Keeps looking in till he meets my eye, then he disappears. Looks like an old sea-captain, or something.'

'Old sea-captain?' said his wife, putting down her work and turning round. There was a strange hesitating note in her voice. She looked at the window, and at the same instant the head of the captain again appeared above the geraniums, and, meeting her gaze, hastily vanished. Martha Pepper sat still for a moment, and then, rising in a slow, dazed fashion, crossed to the door and opened it. Mermaid Passage was empty!

'See anybody?' quavered Pepper.

His wife shook her head, but in a strangely quiet fashion, and, sitting down, took up her knitting again.

For some time the click of the needles and the tick of the clock were the only sounds audible, and the ex-pilot had just arrived at the conclusion that his friend had abandoned him to his fate, when there came a low tapping at the door.

'Come in!' cried Pepper, starting.

The door opened slowly, and the tall figure of Captain Crippen entered and stood there eyeing them nervously. A neat little speech he had prepared failed him at the supreme moment. He leaned against the wall, and in a clumsy, shame-faced fashion lowered his gaze, and stammered out the one word—'Martha!'

At the word Mrs Pepper rose and stood with parted lips, eyeing him wildly.

'Jem!' she gasped, 'Jem!'

'Martha!' croaked the captain again.

With a choking cry Mrs Pepper ran towards him, and, to the huge gratification of her lawful spouse, flung her arms around his neck and kissed him violently.

'Jem,' she cried breathlessly, 'is it really you? I can hardly believe it. Where have you been all this long time? Where have you been?'

'Lots of places,' said the captain, who was not prepared to answer a question like that off-hand; 'but wherever I've been'—he held up his hand theatrically—'the image of my dear lost wife has been always in front of me.'

'I knew you at once, Jem,' said Mrs Pepper fondly, smoothing the hair back from his forehead. 'Have I altered much?'

'Not a bit,' said Crippen, holding her at arm's length and carefully regarding her. 'You look just the same as the first time I set eyes on you.'

'Where have you been?' wailed Martha Pepper, putting her head on his shoulder.

'When the *Dolphin* went down from under me, and left me fighting with the waves for life and Martha, I was cast ashore on a desert island,' began Crippen fluently. 'There I remained for nearly three years, when I was rescued by a barque bound for New South Wales. There I met a man from Poole who told me you were dead. Having no further interest in the land of my birth, I sailed in Australian waters for many years, and it was only lately that I heard how cruelly

I had been deceived, and that my little flower was still blooming.'

The little flower's head being well down on his shoulder again, the celebrated actor exchanged glances with the worshipping Pepper.

'If only you'd come before, Jem,' said Mrs Pepper. 'Who was he? What was his name?'

'Smith,' said the cautious captain.

'If only you'd come before, Jem,' said Mrs Pepper, in a smothered voice, 'it would have been better. Only three months ago I married that object over there.'

The captain attempted a melodramatic start with such success, that, having somewhat underestimated the weight of his fair bride, he nearly lost his balance.

'It can't be helped, I suppose,' he said reproachfully, 'but you might have waited a little longer, Martha.'

'Well, I'm your wife, anyhow,' said Martha, 'and I'll take care I never lose you again. You shall never go out of my sight again till you die. Never.'

'Nonsense, my pet,' said the captain, exchanging uneasy glances with the ex-pilot. 'Nonsense.'

'It isn't nonsense, Jem,' said the lady, as she drew him on to the sofa, and sat with her arms round his neck. 'It may be true, all you've told me, and it may not. For all I know, you may have been married to some other woman; but I've got you now, and I intend to keep you.'

'There, there,' said the captain, as soothingly as a strange sinking at the heart would allow him.

'As for that other little man, I only married him because he worried me so,' said Mrs Pepper tearfully. 'I never loved him, but he used to follow me about and propose ... Was it twelve or thirteen times you proposed to me, Pepper?'

'I forget,' said the ex-pilot shortly.

'But I never loved him,' she continued. 'I never loved you a bit, did I, Pepper?'

'Not a bit,' said Pepper warmly. 'No man could ever have a harder or more unfeeling wife than you. I'll say that for you, willingly.'

As he bore this testimony to his wife's fidelity, there was a knock at the door, and, upon his opening it, the rector's daughter, a lady of uncertain age, entered, and stood regarding with amazement the frantic but ineffectual struggles of Captain Crippen to release himself from a position as uncomfortable as it was ridiculous.

'Mrs Pepper!' said the lady, aghast. 'Oh, Mrs Pepper!'

'It's all right, Miss Winthrop,' said the lady addressed, calmly, as she forced the captain's flushed face on to her ample shoulder again; 'it's my first husband, Jem Budd.'

'Good gracious!' said Miss Winthrop, starting. 'Enoch Arden in the flesh!'

'Who?' inquired Pepper, with a show of polite interest.

'Enoch Arden,' said Miss Winthrop. 'One of our great poets wrote a noble poem about a sailor who came home and found that his wife had married again; but, in the *poem*, the first husband went away without making himself known, and died of a broken heart.'

She looked as Captain Crippen as though he hadn't quite come up to her expectations.

'And now,' said Pepper, speaking with great cheerfulness, 'it's me who has to have the broken heart. Well, well.'

'It's a most interesting case,' cried Miss Winthrop; 'and, if you wait till I fetch my camera, I'll take your portrait together just as you are.'

'Do,' said Mrs Pepper cordially.

'I won't have my portrait taken,' said the captain, with much acerbity.

'Not if I wish it, dear?' inquired Mrs Pepper tenderly.

'Not if you keep wishing it all your life,' replied the captain sourly, making another attempt to get his head from her shoulder.

'Don't you think they ought to have their portrait taken now?' asked Miss Winthrop, turning to the ex-pilot.

'I don't see any harm in it,' said Pepper thoughtlessly.

'You hear what Mr Pepper says,' said the lady, turning to the captain again. 'Surely if he doesn't mind, you ought not to.'

'I'll talk to him by and by,' said the captain, very grimly.

'Perhaps it would be better if we kept this affair to ourselves for the present,' said the ex-pilot, taking alarm at his friend's manner.

'Well, I won't intrude on you any longer,' said Miss Winthrop. 'Oh! Look there! How rude of them!'

The others turned hastily in time to see several heads vanish from the window. Captain Crippen was the first to speak.

'Jem!' said Mrs Pepper severely, before he had finished.

'Captain Budd!' said Miss Winthrop, flushing.

The incensed captain rose to his feet and paced up and down the room. He looked at the ex-pilot, and that small schemer shivered.

'Easy does it, cap'n,' he murmured, with a wink which he meant to be comforting.

'I'm going out a little way,' said the captain, after the rector's daughter had gone. 'Just to cool my head.'

Mrs Pepper took her bonnet from its peg behind the door, and, surveying herself in the glass, tied it beneath her chin.

'Alone,' said Crippen nervously. 'I want to do a little thinking.'

'Never again, Jem,' said Mrs Pepper firmly. 'My place is by your side. If you're ashamed of people looking at you, I'm not. I'm proud of you. Come along. Come and show yourself, and tell them who you are. You shall never go out of my sight again as long as I live. Never.'

She began to whimper.

'What's to be done?' inquired Crippen, turning desperately on the bewildered pilot.

'What's it got to do with him?' demanded Mrs Pepper sharply.

'He's got to be considered a little, I suppose,' said the captain, dissembling. 'Besides, I think I'd better do as the man in the poem did. Let me go away and die of a broken heart. Perhaps it's best.'

Mrs Pepper looked at him with kindling eyes.

'Let me go away and die of a broken heart,' repeated the captain, with real feeling. 'I'd rather do it. I would indeed.'

Mrs Pepper, bursting into angry tears, flung her arms round his neck again, and sobbed on his shoulder. The pilot, obeying the frenzied injunctions of his friend's eye, drew down the blind.

'There's quite a crowd outside,' he remarked.

'I don't mind,' said his wife amiably. 'They'll soon know who he is.'

She stood holding the captain's hand and stroking it, and whenever his feelings became too much for her put her head down on his waistcoat. At such times the captain glared fiercely at the ex-pilot, who, being of a weak nature, was unable, despite his anxiety, to give his faculties that control which the solemnity of the occasion demanded.

The afternoon wore slowly away. Miss Winthrop, who disliked scandal, had allowed something of the affair to leak out, and several visitors, including a local reporter, called, but were put off till the morrow, on the not unnatural plea that the long-separated couple desired a little privacy. The three sat silent, the ex-pilot, with wrinkled brows, trying hard to decipher the lip-language in which the captain addressed him whenever he had an opportunity, but could only dimly guess its purport, when the captain pressed his huge fist into service as well.

Mrs Pepper rose at length, and went into the back room to

prepare tea. As she left the door open, however, and took the captain's hat with her, he built no hopes on her absence, but turned furiously to the ex-pilot.

'What's to be done?' he inquired in a fierce whisper. 'This can't go on.'

'It'll have to,' whispered the other.

'Now look here,' said Crippen menacingly, 'I'm going into the kitchen to make a clean breast of it. I'm sorry for you, but I've done the best I can. Come and help me explain.'

He turned to the kitchen, but the other, with the strength born of despair, seized him by the sleeve and held him back.

'She'll kill me,' he whispered breathlessly.

'I can't help it,' said Crippen, shaking him off. 'Serve you right.'

'And she'll tell the folks outside, and they'll kill you,' continued Pepper.

The captain sat down again, and confronted him with a face as pale as his own.

'The last train leaves at eight,' whispered the pilot hurriedly. 'It's desperate, but it's the only thing you can do. Take her for a stroll up by the fields near the railway station. You can see the train coming in for a mile before it reaches the station. Time yourself carefully, and make a bolt for it. She can't run.'

The entrance of their victim with the tea-tray stopped the conversation; but the captain nodded acceptance behind her back, and then, with a forced gaiety, sat down to tea.

For the first time since his successful appearance he became loquacious, and spoke so freely of incidents in the life of the man he was impersonating that the ex-pilot sat in a perfect fever lest he should blunder. The meal finished, he proposed a stroll, and, as the unsuspecting Mrs Pepper tied on her bonnet, slapped his leg, and winked confidently at his fellow-conspirator.

'I'm not much of a walker,' said the innocent Mrs Pepper, 'so you must go slowly.'

The captain nodded, and at Pepper's suggestion left by the back way, to avoid the gaze of the curious.

For some time after their departure Pepper sat smoking, with his anxious face turned to the clock, until at length, unable to endure the strain any longer, and not without a sportsmanlike idea of being in at the death, he made his way to the station, and placed himself behind a convenient coal-truck.

He waited impatiently, with his eyes fixed on the road up which he expected the captain to come. He looked at his watch. Five minutes to eight, and still no captain. The platform began to fill, a porter seized the big bell and rang it lustily; in the distance a patch of white smoke showed. Just as the watcher had given up all hope, the figure of the captain came in sight. He was swaying from side to side, holding his hat in his hand, but doggedly racing the train to the station.

'He'll never do it!' groaned the pilot. Then he held his breath, for three or four hundred yards behind the captain Mrs Pepper pounded in pursuit.

The train rolled into the station; passengers stepped in and out; doors slammed, and the guard had already placed the whistle in his mouth, when Captain Crippen, breathing stertorously, came stumbling blindly on to the platform, and was hustled into a third-class carriage.

'Close shave that, sir,' said the station-master as he closed the door.

The captain sank back in his seat, fighting for breath, and turning his head, gave a last triumphant look up the road.

'All right, sir,' said the station-master kindly, as he followed the direction of the other's eyes and caught sight of Mrs Pepper. 'We'll wait for your lady.'

Jackson Pepper came from behind the coal-truck and watched the train out of sight, wondering in a dull, vague fashion what the conversation was like. He stood so long that a tender-hearted porter, who had heard the news, made bold to come up and put a friendly hand on his shoulder.

'You'll never see her again, Mr Pepper,' said he sympathetically.

The ex-pilot turned and regarded him fixedly, and the last bit of spirit he was ever known to show flashed up in his face as he spoke.

'You're a blamed idiot!' he said rudely.

A Case of Desertion

THE sun was just rising as the small tub-like steamer, or, to be more correct, steam-barge, the *Bulldog*, steamed past the sleeping town of Gravesend at a good six knots per hour.

There had been a little discussion on the way between her crew and the engineer, who, down in his grimy little engine-room, did his own stoking and everything else necessary. The crew, consisting of captain, mate, and boy, who were doing their first strip on a steamer, had been transferred at the last moment from their sailing-barge the *Witch*, and found to their discomfort that the engineer, who had not expected to sail so soon, was terribly and abusively drunk. Every moment he could spare from his engines he thrust the upper part of his body through the small hatchway, and rowed with his commander.

'Ahoy, bargee!' he shouted, popping up like a jack-in-the-box, after a brief cessation of hostilities.

'Don't take any notice of him,' said the mate. 'He's got a bottle of brandy down there, and he's half mad.'

'If I knew anything about those engines,' growled the skipper, 'I'd go and hit him over the head.'

'But you don't,' said the mate, 'and neither do I, so you'd better keep quiet.'

'You think you're a fine fellow,' continued the engineer, 'standing up there and playing with that little wheel. You think you're doing all the work. What's that boy doing? Send him down to stoke.'

'Go down,' said the skipper, glaring with fury, and the boy reluctantly obeyed.

'You think,' said the engineer pathetically, after he had cuffed the boy's head and dropped him down below by the scruff of his neck, 'you think because I've got a dirty face I'm not a man. There's many an oily face hides a good heart.'

'I don't think anything about it,' grunted the skipper; 'you do your work, and I'll do mine.'

'Don't you give me any of your back answers,' bellowed the engineer, ''cos I won't have them.'

The skipper shrugged his shoulders and exchanged glances with his sympathetic mate. 'Wait till I get him ashore,' he murmured.

'The boiler is worn out,' said the engineer, reappearing after a hasty dive below. 'It may burst at any moment.'

As though to confirm his words fearful sounds were heard proceeding from below.

'It's only the boy,' said the mate, 'he's scared—naturally.'

'I thought it was the boiler,' said the skipper, with a sigh of relief. 'It was loud enough.'

As he spoke the boy got his head out of the hatchway, and, rendered desperate with fear, fairly fought his way past the engineer and gained the deck.

'Very good,' said the engineer, as he followed him on deck and staggered to the side. 'I've had enough of you lot.'

'Hadn't you better go down to those engines?' shouted the skipper.

'Am I your *slave*?' demanded the engineer tearfully. 'Tell me that. Am I your slave?'

'Go down and do your work like a sensible man,' was the reply.

At these words the engineer took umbrage at once, and, scowling fiercely, removed his greasy jacket and flung his cap on the deck. He then finished the brandy which he had brought up with him, and gazed owlishly at the Kentish shore.

'I'm going to have a wash,' he said loudly, and, sitting down, removed his boots.

'Go down to the engines first,' said the skipper, 'and I'll send the boy to you with a bucket and some soap.'

'Bucket!' replied the engineer scornfully, as he moved to the side. 'I'm going to have a proper wash.'

'Hold him!' roared the skipper suddenly. 'Hold him!'

The mate, realizing the situation, rushed to seize him, but the engineer, with a mad laugh, put his hands on the side and vaulted into the water. When he rose the steamer was twenty yards ahead.

'Go astern!' yelled the mate.

'How can I go astern when there's nobody at the engines?' shouted the skipper, as he hung on to the wheel and brought the boat's head sharply round. 'Get a line ready.'

The mate, with a coil of rope in his hand, rushed to the side, but his benevolent efforts were frustrated by the engineer, who, seeing the boat's head making straight for him, saved his life by an opportune dive. The steamer rushed by.

'Turn her again!' screamed the mate.

The captain was already doing so, and in a remarkably short space of time the boat, which had described a complete circle, was making again for the engineer.

'Look out for the line!' shouted the mate warningly.

'I don't want your line,' yelled the engineer. 'I'm going ashore.'

'Come aboard!' shouted the captain imploringly, as they swept past again. 'We can't manage the engines.'

'Put her round again,' said the mate. 'I'll go for him with the boat. Haul her in, boy.'

The boat, which was dragging astern, was hauled close, and the mate tumbled into her, followed by the boy, just as the captain was in the middle of another circle—to the intense indignation of a crowd of shipping, large and small, which was trying to get by.

'Ahoy!' yelled the master of a tug which was towing a large ship. 'Take that steam roundabout out of the way. What in thunder are you doing?'

'Picking up my engineer,' replied the captain, as he steamed right across the other's bows, and nearly ran down a sailing-barge, the skipper of which, a Salvation Army man, was nobly fighting his feelings.

'Why don't you stop?' he yelled.

'Because I can't,' wailed the skipper of the *Bulldog*, as he threaded his way between a huge steamer and a schooner, who, in avoiding him, were getting up a little collision on their own account.

'Ahoy, *Bulldog!* Ahoy!' called the mate. 'Stand by to pick us up. We've got him.'

The skipper smiled in an agonized fashion as he shot past, hotly pursued by his boat. The feeling on board the other craft as they got out of the way of the *Bulldog*, and nearly ran down her boat, and then, in avoiding that, nearly ran down something else, cannot be put into plain English, but several captains ventured into the domains of the ornamental with marked success.

'Shut off steam!' yelled the engineer, as the *Bulldog* went by again. 'Draw the fires, then.'

'Who's going to steer while I do it?' bellowed the skipper, as he left the wheel for a few seconds to try and get a line to throw them.

By this time the commotion in the river was frightful, and the captain's steering, as he went on his round again, was something marvellous to behold. A strange lack of sympathy on the part of brother captains added to his troubles. Every craft he passed had something to say to him, busy as they were, and the remarks were as monotonous as they were insulting. At last, just as he was resolving to run his boat straight down the river until he came to a halt for want of steam, the mate caught the rope he flung, and the *Bulldog* went down the river with her boat made fast to her stern.

'Come aboard, you—you lunatic!' he shouted.

'Not before I know how I stand,' said the engineer, who was now beautifully sober, and in full possession of a somewhat acute intellect.

'What do you mean?' demanded the skipper.

'I don't come aboard,' shouted the engineer, 'until you and the mate and the boy all swear that you won't say anything about this little game.'

'I'll report you the moment I get ashore,' roared the skipper. 'I'll give you in charge for desertion. I'll——'

With a supreme gesture the engineer prepared to dive, but the watchful mate fell on his neck and tripped him over a seat.

'Come aboard!' said the skipper, aghast at such determination. 'Come aboard, and I'll give you a licking when we get ashore instead.'

'Honour bright?' inquired the engineer.

'Honour bright,' chorused the three.

The engineer, with all the honours of war, came on board, and, after remarking that he felt chilly bathing on an empty stomach, went down below and began to stoke. In the course of the voyage he said that it was worth while making such a fool of himself if only to see the skipper's beautiful steering, warmly asseverating that there was not another man on the river that could have done it. Before this insidious flattery the skipper's wrath melted like snow before the sun, and by the time they reached port he would as soon have thought of hitting his own father as his smooth-tongued engineer.

Outsailed

IT was a momentous occasion. The two skippers sat in the private bar of the Old Ship, in High Street, Wapping, solemnly sipping cold gin and smoking cigars, whose sole merit consisted in the fact that they had been smuggled. It is well known all along the waterside that this greatly improves their flavour.

'Draw all right?' queried Captain Berrow—a short, fat man of few ideas, who was the exulting owner of a bundle of them.

'Beautiful,' replied Captain Tucker, who had just made an excursion into the interior of his with the small blade of his penknife. 'Why don't you keep smokes like these, landlord?'

'He can't,' chuckled Captain Berrow fatuously. 'They're not to be had—money couldn't buy them.'

The landlord grunted. 'Why don't you settle about that race of yours and have done with it,' he cried, as he wiped down his counter. 'Seems to me, Cap'n Tucker's hanging fire.'

'I'm ready when he is,' said Tucker, somewhat shortly.

'It's taking your money,' said Berrow slowly; 'the *Thistle* can't hold a candle to the *Good Intent*, and you know it. Many a time that little schooner of mine has kept up with a steamer.'

'Where would you have been if the tow rope had parted though?' said the master of the *Thistle*, with a wink at the landlord.

At this remark Captain Berrow took fire, and, with his temper rapidly rising to fever heat, wrathfully repelled the scurvy insinuation in language which compelled the respectful attention of all the other customers and the hasty intervention of the landlord.

'Put up the stakes,' he cried impatiently. 'Put up the stakes, and don't have so much jaw about it.'

'Here's mine,' said Berrow, sturdily handing over a greasy five-pound note. 'Now, Cap'n Tucker, cover that.'

'Come on,' said the landlord encouragingly; 'don't let him take the wind out of your sails like that.'

Tucker handed over five sovereigns.

'High water's at 12.13,' said the landlord, pocketing the stakes. 'You understand the conditions—each of you does the best he can for himself after eleven, and the one who gets to Poole first has the ten pounds. Understand?'

Both gamblers breathed hard, and, fully realizing the desperate nature of the enterprise upon which they had embarked, ordered some more gin. A rivalry of long standing as to the merits of their respective schooners had led to them calling in the landlord to arbitrate, and this was the result. Berrow, vaguely feeling that it would be advisable to keep on good terms with the stakeholder, offered him one of the famous cigars. The stakeholder, anxious to keep on good terms with his stomach, declined it.

'You've both got your moorings up, I suppose?' he inquired.

'Got them up this evening,' replied Tucker. 'We're just made fast one each side of the *Dolphin* now.'

'The wind's light, but it's from the right quarter,' said Captain Berrow, 'and I only hope that the best ship'll win. I'd like to win myself, but, if not, I can only say there's no man

156

breathing I'd sooner have lick me than Cap'n Tucker. He's as smart a seaman as ever comes into the London river, and he's got a schooner angels would be proud of.'

'Glasses of gin all round,' said Tucker promptly. 'Cap'n Berrow, here's your very good health, and a fair field and no favour.'

With these praiseworthy sentiments the master of the *Thistle* finished his liquor, and, wiping his mouth on the back of his hand, nodded farewell to others and departed. Once in the High Street he walked slowly, as one in deep thought, then, with a sudden resolution, turned up Nightingale Lane, and made for a small unsavoury thoroughfare leading out of Ratcliff Highway. A quarter of an hour later he emerged into that famous thoroughfare again, smiling incoherently, and, retracting his steps to the waterside, jumped into a boat, and was pulled off to his ship.

'Comes off tonight, Joe,' said he, as he descended to the cabin, 'and it's ten bob to you if the old girl wins.'

'What's the bet?' inquired the mate, looking up from his task of shredding tobacco.

'Five pounds,' replied the skipper.

'Well, we ought to do it,' said the mate slowly; 'it won't be my fault if we don't.'

'Nor mine,' said the skipper. 'As a matter of fact, Joe, I reckon I've about made sure of it. All's fair in love and war and racing, Joe.'

'Ay, ay,' said the mate, more slowly than before, as he revolved this addition to the proverb.

'I just nipped round and saw a chap I used to know named Dibbs,' said the skipper. 'Keeps a boarding-house for sailors. Wonderful sharp little chap he is. Needles aren't anything to him. There's heaps of needles, but only one Dibbs. He's going to make old Berrow's chaps as drunk as lords.'

'Does he know them?' inquired the mate.

'He knows where to find them,' said the other. 'I told him

they'd either be in the Duke's Head or the Town of Berwick. But he'll find them wherever they are. Yes, even if they were in a coffee house, I believe that man would find them.'

'They're steady chaps,' objected the mate, but in a weak fashion, being somewhat staggered by this tribute to Mr Dibbs's remarkable powers.

'My lad,' said the skipper, 'it's Dibbs's business to mix sailors' liquor so's they don't know whether they're standing on their heads or their heels. Many a sailorman has got up a ship's side, thinking it was stairs and gone off half across the world instead of going to bed, through him.'

'We'll have an easy job of it, then,' said the mate. 'I believe we could have managed it without that, though. T'isn't quite what you'd call sport, is it?'

'There's nothing like making sure of a thing,' said the skipper placidly. 'What time are our chaps coming aboard?'

'Ten thirty, the latest,' replied the mate. 'Old Sam's with them, so they'll be all right.'

'I'll turn in for a couple of hours,' said the skipper, going towards his berth. 'I'd give something to see old Berrow's face as his chaps come up the side.'

'Perhaps they won't get as far as that,' remarked the mate.

'Oh, yes they will,' said the skipper. 'Dibbs is going to see to that. I don't want any chance of the race being scratched. Turn me out in a couple of hours.'

He closed the door behind him, and the mate, having stuffed his clay pipe with the coarse tobacco, took some pink note-paper with scalloped edges from his drawer, and, placing the paper at his right side, and squaring his shoulders, began some private correspondence.

For some time he smoked and wrote in silence, until the increasing darkness warned him to finish his task. He signed the note, and, having put a few marks of a tender nature below his signature, sealed it ready for the post, and sat with half-closed eyes, finishing his pipe. Then his head nodded, and, placing his arms on the table, he too slept.

It seemed but a minute since he had closed his eyes when he was awakened by the entrance of the skipper, who came blundering into the darkness from his stateroom, vociferating loudly and nervously.

'Ay, ay!' said Joe, starting up.

'Where's the lights?' said the skipper. 'What's the time? I dreamt I'd overslept. What's the time?'

'Plenty of time,' said the mate vaguely, as he stifled a yawn.

'Half-past ten,' said the skipper, as he struck a match. 'You've been asleep,' he added severely.

'I haven't,' said the mate stoutly, as he followed the other on deck. 'I've been thinking. I think better in the dark.'

'It's about time our chaps were aboard,' said the skipper, as he looked round the deserted deck. 'I hope they won't be late.'

'Sam's with 'em,' said the mate confidently, as he went on to the side; 'there aren't any festivities going on aboard the *Good Intent*, either.'

'There will be,' said his worthy skipper, with a grin, as he looked across the intervening brig at the rival craft; 'there will be.'

He walked round the deck to see that everything was snug and ship-shape, and got back to the mate just as a howl of surprising weirdness was heard proceeding from the neighbouring stairs.

'I'm surprised at Berrow allowing his men to make that noise,' said the skipper waggishly. 'Our chaps are there too, I think. I can hear Sam's voice.'

'So can I,' said the mate, with emphasis.

'Seems to be talking rather loud,' said the master of the *Thistle*, knitting his brows.

'Sounds as though he's trying to sing,' said the mate, as,

after some delay, a heavily-laden boat put off from the stairs and made slowly for them. 'No, he isn't; he's screaming.'

There was no longer any doubt about it. The respectable and greatly-trusted Sam was letting off a series of wild howls which would have done credit to a Zulu warrior, and was evidently very much out of temper about something.

'Ahoy, *Thistle!* Ahoy!' bellowed the waterman, as he neared the schooner. 'Throw a rope—quick!'

The mate threw him one, and the boat came alongside. It was then seen that another waterman, using impatient and deplorable language, was forcibly holding Sam down in the boat.

'What's he done? What's the row?' demanded the mate.

'Done?' said the waterman, in disgust. 'Done? He's had a small lemon, and it's gone to his silly old head. He's making all this fuss 'cos he wanted to set the pub on fire, and they wouldn't let him. Man ashore told us they belonged to the *Good Intent*, but I know they're your men.'

'Sam!' roared the skipper, with a sinking heart, as his glance fell on the recumbent figures in the boat; 'come aboard at once, you drunken disgrace! D'you hear?'

'I can't leave him,' said Sam, whimpering.

'Leave who?' growled the skipper.

'Him,' said Sam, placing his arms round the waterman's neck. 'He's like my brother.'

'Get up, you old lunatic!' snarled the waterman, extricating himself with difficulty, and forcing the other towards the side. 'Now, up you go!'

Aided by the shoulders of the waterman and the hands of his superior officers, Sam went up, and then the waterman turned his attention to the remainder of his fares, who were snoring contentedly in the bottom of the boat.

'Now then!' he cried; 'look alive with you! D'you hear? Wake up! Wake up!'

'What the devil's the matter with them?' stormed the

160

master of the *Thistle*. 'Throw a pail of water over them, Joe!'

Joe obeyed with gusto, and, as he never had much of a head for details, bestowed most of it upon the watermen. Through the row which ensued the *Thistle's* crew snored peacefully, and at last were handed up over the sides like sacks of potatoes, and the indignant watermen pulled back to the stairs.

'Here's a nice crew to win a race with!' wailed the skipper, almost crying with rage. 'Throw the water over them, Joe! Throw the water over them!'

Joe obeyed willingly, until at length, to the skipper's great relief, one man stirred, and, sitting up on the deck, sleepily expressed his firm conviction that it was raining. For a moment they both had hopes of him, but as Joe went to the side for another bucketful, he evidently came to the conclusion that he had been dreaming, and, lying down again, resumed his nap. As he did so, the first stroke of Big Ben came booming down the river.

'Eleven o'clock!' shouted the excited skipper.

It was too true. Before Big Ben had finished, the neighbouring church clocks commenced striking with feverish haste, and hurrying feet and hoarse cries were heard proceeding from the deck of the *Good Intent*.

'Loose the sails!' yelled the furious Tucker. 'Loose the sails! We'll have to get under way by ourselves!'

He ran forward, and, assisted by the mate, hoisted the jibs, and then, running back, cast off from the brig, and began to hoist the mainsail. As they disengaged themselves from the tier, there was just sufficient sail for them to advance against the tide; while in front of them the *Good Intent*, shaking out sail after sail, stood boldly down the river.

'This was the way of it,' said Sam, as he stood before the grim Tucker at six o'clock the next morning, surrounded by his mates. 'He came into the Town of Berwick, where we were, as nice spoken a little chap as ever you'd wish to see. He said he's been looking at the *Good Intent*, and he thought it was the prettiest little craft he ever saw, and the exact image of one his brother, who was a missionary, had, and he'd like to stand a drink to every man of her crew. Of course, we said we were the crew at once, and all I can remember after that is two policemen and a little boy trying to frog-march me, and somebody throwing pails of water over me. It's very hard losing a race, which we didn't know anything about, in this way; but it wasn't our fault—it wasn't indeed. It's my belief that the little man was a missionary of some sort himself, and wanted to convert us, and that was his way of starting on the job. It's all very well for the mate to have hysterics; but it's quite true, every word of it, and if you go and ask at the pub they'll tell you the same.'

Mated

THE schooner *Falcon* was ready for sea. The last bale of general cargo had just been shipped, and a few hairy, unkempt seamen were busy putting on the hatches under the able supervision of the mate.

'All clear?' inquired the master, a short, ruddy-faced man of about thirty-five. 'Cast off there!'

'Aren't you going to wait for the passengers?' inquired the mate.

'No, no,' replied the skipper, whose features were working with excitement. 'They won't come now, I'm sure they won't. We'll lose the tide if we don't look sharp.'

He turned aside to give an order just as a buxom young woman, accompanied by a loutish boy, a band-box, and several other bundles, came hurrying on to the jetty.

'Well, here we are Cap'n Evans,' said the girl, springing lightly on to the deck. 'I thought we should never get here; the cabman didn't seem to know the way; but I knew you wouldn't go without us.'

'Here you are,' said the skipper, with attempted cheerfulness, as he gave the girl his right hand, while his left strayed vaguely in the direction of the boy's ear, which was coldly withheld from him. 'Go down below, and the mate'll show you your cabin. Bill, this is Miss Cooper, a lady friend of mine, and her brother.'

The mate, acknowledging the introduction, led the way to the cabin, where they remained so long that by the time they came on deck again the schooner was off Limehouse, slipping along well under a light wind.

'How do you like the state-room?' inquired the skipper, who was at the wheel.

'Pretty fair,' replied Miss Cooper. 'It's a big name for it though, isn't it? Oh, what a large ship!'

She ran to the side to gaze at a big liner, and as far as Gravesend besieged the skipper and mate with questions concerning the various craft. At the mate's suggestion they had tea on deck, at which meal William Henry Cooper became a source of much discomfort to his host by his remarkable discoveries anent the fauna of lettuce. Despite his efforts, however, and the cloud under which Evans seemed to be labouring, the meal was voted a big success; and after it was over they sat laughing and chatting until the air got chilly, and the banks of the river were lost in the gathering darkness. At ten o'clock they retired for the night, leaving Evans and the mate on deck.

'Nice girl, that,' said the mate, looking at the skipper, who was leaning moodily on the wheel.

'Ay, ay,' replied he. 'Bill,' he continued, turning suddenly towards the mate. 'I'm in an awful mess. You've got a good square head on your shoulders. Now, what on earth am I to do? Of course you can see how the land lies?'

'Of course,' said the mate, who was not going to lose his reputation by any display of ignorance. 'Anyone could see it,' he added.

'The question is what's to be done?' said the skipper.

'That's the question,' said the mate guardedly.

'I feel so worried,' said Evans, 'that I've actually thought of getting into collision, or running the ship ashore. Fancy those two women meeting at Llandalock.'

Such a sudden light broke in upon the square head of the mate, that he nearly whistled with the brightness of it.

'But you aren't *engaged* to this one?' he cried.

'We're to be married in August,' said the skipper desperately. 'That's my ring on her finger.'

'But you're going to marry Mary Jones in September,' expostulated the mate. 'You can't marry both of them.'

'That's what I say,' replied Evans; 'that's what I keep telling myself, but it doesn't seem to bring much comfort. I'm too soft-hearted where women are concerned, Bill, and that's the truth of it. Directly I get alongside a nice girl my arm goes creeping round her before I know what it's doing.'

'What on earth made you bring the girl on the ship?' inquired the mate. 'The other one's sure to be on the quay to meet you as usual.'

'I couldn't help it,' groaned the skipper; 'she would come; she can be very determined when she likes. She's awfully gone on me, Bill.'

'So's the other one apparently,' said the mate.

'I can't think what it is the girls see in me,' said the other mournfully. 'Can you?'

'No, I certainly can't,' replied the mate frankly.

'I don't take any credit for it, Bill,' said the skipper, 'not a bit. My father was like it before me. The worry's killing me.'

'Well, which are you going to have?' inquired the mate. 'Which do you like the best?'

'I don't know, and that's a fact,' said the skipper. 'They've both got money coming to them; when I'm in Wales I like Mary Jones best, and when I'm in London it's Janey Cooper. It's dreadful to be like that, Bill.'

'It is,' said the mate dryly. 'I wouldn't be in your shoes when those two girls meet. Then you'll have old Jones and her brothers to tackle, too. Seems to me things will be a bit lively.'

'I have thought of being taken sick, and staying in my bunk, Bill,' suggested Evans anxiously.

'And have the two of them nursing you,' retorted Bill. 'Nice quiet time for an invalid.'

Evans made a gesture of despair.

'How would it be,' said the mate, after a long pause, and speaking very slowly; 'how would it be if I took this one off your hands.'

'You couldn't do it, Bill,' said the skipper decidedly. 'Not while she knew I was above ground.'

'Well, I can try,' returned the mate shortly. 'I've taken rather a fancy to the girl. Is it a bargain?'

'It is,' said the skipper, shaking hands upon it. 'If you get me out of this hole, Bill, I'll remember it as long as I live.'

With these words he went below, and, after cautiously undoing W. H. Cooper, who had slept himself into a knot that a professional contortionist would have envied, tumbled in beside him and went to sleep.

His heart almost failed him when he encountered the radiant Jane at breakfast the next morning, but he concealed his feelings with a strong effort. After the meal was finished and the passengers had gone on deck, he got hold of the mate, who was following, and drew him into the cabin.

'You haven't washed yourself this morning,' he said, eyeing him closely. 'How do you suppose you are going to make an impression if you don't look smart?'

'Well, I look tidier than you do,' growled the mate.

'Of course you do,' said the wily Evans. 'I'm going to give you all the chances I can. Now you go and shave, and here— take it.'

He passed the surprised mate a brilliant red silk tie, embellished with green spots.

'No, no,' said the mate deprecatingly.

'Take it,' said Evans; 'if anything'll fetch her it'll be that

166

tie; and here's a couple of collars for you; they're a new shape, quite the rage down Poplar way just now.'

'It's robbing you,' said the mate, 'and it's no good either. I haven't got a decent suit of clothes to my name.'

Evans looked up, and their eyes met; then, with a catch in his breath, he turned away, and after some hesitation went to his locker, and bringing out a new suit, bought for the edification of Miss Jones, handed it silently to the mate.

'I can't take all these things without giving you something for them,' said the mate. 'Here, wait a bit.'

He dived into his cabin, and, after a hasty search, brought out some garments which he placed on the table before his commander.

'I wouldn't wear them, not even to drown myself in,' declared Evans after a brief glance; 'they aren't even decent.'

'So much the better,' said the mate; 'it'll be more of a contrast to me.'

After a slight contest the skipper gave way, and the mate, after an elaborate toilet, went on deck and began to make himself agreeable, while his chief skulked below trying to muster up courage to put in an appearance.

'Where's the captain?' inquired Miss Cooper, after his absence had been so prolonged as to become noticeable.

'He's below, dressing, I believe,' replied the mate simply.

Miss Cooper, glancing at his attire, smiled softly to herself, and prepared for something startling, and she got it. A more forlorn, sulky-looking object than the skipper, when he did appear, had never been seen on the deck of the *Falcon*, and his London betrothed glanced at him hot with shame and indignation.

'Whatever have you got those things on for?' she whispered.

'Work, my dear—work,' replied the skipper.

'Well, mind you don't lose any of the pieces,' said the "dear" suavely; 'you might not be able to match that cloth.'

'I'll look after that,' said the skipper, reddening. 'You must excuse me talking to you now. I'm busy.'

Miss Cooper looked at him indignantly, and, biting her lip, turned away, and started a desperate flirtation with the mate, to punish him. Evans watched them with mingled feelings as he busied himself with various small jobs on the deck, his wrath being raised to boiling point by the behaviour of the cook, who, being a poor hand at disguising his feelings, came out of the galley several times to look at him.

From this incident a coolness sprang up between the skipper and the girl, which increased hourly. At times the skipper weakened, but the watchful mate was always on hand to prevent mischief. Owing to his fostering care Evans was generally busy, and always gruff; and Miss Cooper, who was used to the most assiduous attentions from him, didn't know whether to be bewildered or indignant. Four times in one day he remarked in her hearing that a sailor's ship was his sweetheart, while his treatment of his small prospective brother-in-law, when he expostulated with him on the state of his wardrobe, filled that hitherto pampered youth with amazement. At last, on the fourth night out, as the little schooner was passing the coast of Cornwall, the mate came up to him as he was steering, and patted him heavily on the back.

'It's all right, cap'n,' said he. 'You've lost the prettiest little girl in England.'

'What?' said the skipper, in incredulous tones.

'Fact,' said the other. 'Here's your ring back. I wouldn't let her wear it any longer.'

'However did you do it?' inquired Evans, taking the ring in a dazed fashion.

'Oh, easy as possible,' said the mate. 'She liked me best, that's all.'

'But what did you say to her?' persisted Evans.

The other reflected.

'I can't call to mind exactly,' he said at length. 'But, you may

168

rely upon it, I said everything I could against you. But she never did care much for you. She told me so herself.'

'I wish you joy of your bargain,' said Evans solemnly, after a long pause.

'What do you mean?' demanded the mate sharply.

'A girl like that,' said the skipper, with a lump in his throat, 'who can carry on with two men at once isn't worth having. She's not my money, that's all.'

The mate looked at him in honest bewilderment.

'Mark my words,' continued the skipper loftily, 'you'll live to regret it. A girl like that's got no ballast. She'll always be running after fresh neckties.'

'You put it down to the necktie, do you?' sneered the mate wrathfully.

'That and the clothes, certainly,' replied the skipper.

'Well, you're wrong,' said the mate. 'A lot you know about girls. It wasn't your old clothes, and it wasn't all your bad behaviour to her since she's been aboard. You may as well know first as last. She wouldn't have anything to do with me at first, so I told her all about Mary Jones.'

'You told her *that*?' cried the skipper fiercely.

'I did,' replied the other. 'She was pretty wild at first; but then the comic side of it struck her—you wearing those old clothes, and going about as you did. She used to watch you until she couldn't stand it any longer, and then go down in the cabin and laugh. Wonderful spirits that girl's got. Hush! here she is!'

As he spoke the girl came on deck, and, seeing the two men talking together, remained a short distance from them.

'It's all right, Jane,' said the mate; 'I've told him.'

'Oh!' said Miss Cooper, with a little gasp.

'I can't bear deceit,' said the mate; 'and now it's off his mind, he's so happy he can't bear himself.'

The latter part of this assertion seemed to be more warranted by facts than the former, but Evans made a choking noise, which he intended as a sign of unbearable joy, and, relinquishing the wheel to the mate, walked forward. The clear sky was thick with stars, and a mind at ease might have found enjoyment in the quiet beauty of the night, but the skipper was too interested in the behaviour of the young couple at the wheel to give it a thought. Immersed in each other, they forgot him entirely, and exchanged playful little slaps and pushes, which incensed him beyond description. Several times he was on the point of exercising his position as commander and ordering the mate below, but in the circumstances interference was impossible, and, with a low-voiced good night, he went below. Here his gaze fell on William Henry, who was slumbering peacefully, and, with a hazy idea of the eternal fitness of things, he raised the youth in his arms, and, despite his sleepy protests, deposited him in the mate's bunk. Then, with head and heart both aching, he retired for the night.

There was a little embarrassment next day, but it soon passed off, and the three adult inmates of the cabin got on quite easy terms with each other. The most worried person aft was the boy, who had not been taken into their confidence, and whose face, when his sister sat with the mate's arm around her waist, presented to the skipper a perfect study in emotions.

'I feel quite curious to see this Miss Jones,' said Miss Cooper amiably, as they sat at dinner.

'She'll be on the quay, waving her handkerchief to him,' said the mate. 'We'll be in tomorrow afternoon, and then you'll see her.'

As it happened, the mate was a few hours out in his reckoning, for by the time the *Falcon's* bows were laid for the small harbour it was quite dark, and the little schooner glided in, guided by the two lights which marked the entrance. The quay, seen in the light of a few scattered lamps, looked dreary enough, and, except for two or three indistinct figures, appeared deserted. Beyond, the broken lights of the town stood out more clearly as the schooner crept slowly over the dark water towards her berth.

'Fine night, cap'n,' said the watchman, as the schooner came gently alongside the quay.

The skipper grunted assent. He was peering anxiously at the quay.

'It's too late,' said the mate. 'You couldn't expect her this time of night. It's ten o'clock.'

'I'll go over in the morning,' said Evans, who, now that things had been adjusted, was secretly disappointed that Miss Cooper had not witnessed the meeting. 'If you're not going ashore, we might have a hand of cards as soon as we're made fast.'

The mate assenting, they went below, and were soon deep in the mysteries of three-hand cribbage. Evans, who was a good player, surpassed himself, and had just won the first game, the others being nowhere, when a head was thrust down the companion way, and a voice like a strained foghorn called the captain by name.

'Ay, Ay!' yelled Evans, laying down his hand.

'I'll come down, cap'n,' said the voice, and the mate just had time to whisper 'Old Jones' to Miss Cooper, when a man of mighty bulk filled up the doorway of the little cabin, and extended a huge paw to Evans and the mate. He then looked at the lady, and, breathing hard, waited.

'Young lady of the mate's,' said Evans breathlessly; 'Miss Cooper. Sit down, cap'n. Get the gin out, Bill.'

'Not for me,' said Captain Jones firmly, but with an obvious effort.

The surprise of Evans and the mate admitted of no conceal- ment; but it passed unnoticed by their visitor, who, fidgeting in his seat, appeared to be labouring with some mysterious problem. After a long pause, during which all watched him anxiously, he reached over the table and shook hands with Evans again.

'Put it there, cap'n,' said Evans, much affected by this token of esteem.

The old man rose and stood looking at him, with his hand on his shoulder; he then shook hands for the third time, and patted him encouragingly on the back.

'Is anything the matter?' demanded the skipper of the *Falcon* as he rose to his feet, alarmed by these manifestations of feeling. 'Is Mary—is she ill?'

'Worse than that,' said the other. 'Worse than that, my poor boy; she's married a lobster!'

The effect of this communication upon Evans was tremendous; but it may be doubted whether he was more surprised than Miss Cooper, who, utterly unversed in military terms, strove in vain to realize the possibility of such a *mésalliance*, as she gazed wildly at the speaker and squeaked in astonishment.

'When was it?' asked Evans at last, in a dull voice.

'Thursday fortnight, at half-past eleven,' said the old man. 'He's a sergeant in the line. I would have written to you, but I thought it was best to come and break it to you gently. Cheer up, my boy; there's more than one Mary Jones in the world.'

With this undeniable fact, Captain Jones waved a farewell to the party and went off, leaving them to digest his news. For some time they sat still, the mate and Miss Cooper exchanging whispers, until at length, the stillness becoming oppressive, they withdrew to their respective berths, leaving the skipper sitting at the table, gazing hard at a knot in the opposite locker.

For long after their departure he sat thus, amid a deep silence, broken only by an occasional giggle from the state-room, or an idiotic sniggering from the direction of the mate's bunk, until, recalled to mundane affairs by the lamp burning itself out, he went, in befitting gloom, to bed.

The Rival Beauties

'IF you hadn't asked me,' said the night-watchman, 'I should never have told you; but, seeing as you've put the question point blank, I will tell you my experience of it. You're the first person I've opened my lips to upon the subject, for it was so extraordinary that all our chaps swore they'd keep it to themselves for fear of being disbelieved and jeered at.

'It happened in '84, on board the steamer *George Washington* bound from Liverpool to New York. The first eight days passed without anything unusual happening, but on the ninth I was standing aft with the first mate, hauling in the log, when we heard a yell from aloft, and a chap we called Stuttering Sam came down as if he was possessed, and rushed up to the mate with his eyes nearly starting out of his head.

'"There's the s-s-s-s-s-sis-sis-sip!" says he.

'"The what?" says the mate.

'"The s-s-sea-sea-sssssip!"

'"Look here, my lad," says the mate, taking out a pocket-handkerchief and wiping his face, "you just turn your head away till you get your breath. It's like opening a bottle of soda water to stand talking to you. Now, what is it?"

'"It's the ssssssis-sea-sea-sea-serpent!" says Sam, with a burst.

173

'"Rather a long one by your account of it," says the mate, with a grin.

'"What's the matter?" says the skipper, who just came up.

'"This man has seen the sea-serpent, sir, that's all," says the mate.

'"Y-y-yes," said Sam, with a sort of sob.

'"Well, there isn't much doing just now," says the skipper, "so you'd better get a slice of bread and feed it."

'The mate burst out laughing, and I could see by the way the skipper smiled that he was rather tickled himself.

'The skipper and the mate were still laughing heartily when we heard a dreadful howl from the bridge, and one of the chaps suddenly leaves the wheel, jumps on to the deck, and bolts below as though he was mad. T'other one follows him almost directly, and the second mate caught hold of the wheel as he left it, and called out something we couldn't catch to the skipper.

'"What in thunder is the matter?" yells the skipper.

'The mate pointed to starboard, but his hand was shaking so much that one minute it was pointing to the sky and the next to the bottom of the sea, so wasn't much guide to us. Even when he got it steady we couldn't see anything, till all of a sudden, about two miles off, something like a telegraph pole stuck up out of the water for a few seconds, and then ducked down again and made straight for the ship.

'Sam was the first to speak, and, without wasting time stuttering or stammering, he said he'd go down and see about that bit of bread, and he went before the skipper or the mate could stop him.

'In less than half a minute there were only the three officers and me on deck. The second mate was holding the wheel, the skipper was holding his breath, and the first mate was holding me. It was one of the most exciting times I ever had.

'"Better fire the gun at it," says the skipper, in a trembling voice, looking at the little brass cannon we had for signalling.

'"Better not give him cause for offence," says the mate, shaking his head.

'"I wonder whether it eats men," says the skipper. "Perhaps it'll come for some of us."

'"There aren't many on deck for it to choose from," says the mate, looking at him significantly.

'"That's true," says the skipper, very thoughtfully; "I'll go and send all hands on deck. As captain, it's my duty not to leave the ship till the *last*, if I can anyways help it."

'How he got them on deck has always been a wonder to me, but he did. He was a brutal sort of a man at the best of times, and he carried on so much that I suppose they thought even the serpent couldn't be worse. Anyway, they all came up, and we all stood in a crowd watching the serpent as it came closer and closer.

'We reckoned it to be about a hundred yards long, and it was the most awful-looking creature you could ever imagine. If you took all the ugliest things in the earth and mixed them up—gorillas and the like—you'd only begin to get an idea of what it was like. It just hung off our quarter, keeping up with us, and every now and then it would open its mouth and let us see about four yards down its throat.

'"It seems peaceful," whispers the first mate, after a time.

'"Perhaps it isn't hungry," says the skipper. "We'd better not let it get peckish. Try it with a loaf of bread."

'The cook went below and fetched up half a dozen, and one of the chaps, plucking up courage, slung it over the side, and before you could say "Jack Robinson" the serpent had eaten it up and was looking for more. It stuck its head up and came close to the side just like the swans in Victoria Park, and it kept that game up until it had had ten loaves and a hunk of pork.

'"I'm afraid we're encouraging it," says the skipper, looking at it as it swam alongside with an eye as big as a saucer cocked on the ship.

'"Perhaps it'll go away soon if we don't take any more notice of it," says the mate. "Just pretend it isn't here."

'Well, we did pretend as well as we could; but everybody hugged the port side of the ship, and was ready to bolt down below at the shortest notice; and at last, when the beast got craning its neck up over the side as though it was looking for something, we gave it some more food. We thought if we didn't give it he might take it, and take it off the wrong shelf, so to speak. But, as the mate said, it was encouraging it, and long after it was dark we could hear it snorting and splashing behind us, until at last it had such an effect on us the mate sent one of the chaps down to rouse the skipper.

'"I don't think it'll do any harm," says the skipper, peering over the side, and speaking as though he knew all about sea-serpents and their ways.

'"Suppose it puts its head over the side and takes one of the men," says the mate.

'"Let me know at once," says the skipper firmly; and he went below again and left us.

'Well, I was jolly glad when eight bells struck and I went below; and if ever I hoped anything I hoped that when I went up again that ugly brute would have gone, but, instead of that, when I went on deck it was playing alongside like a kitten almost, and one of the chaps told me that the skipper had been feeding it again.

'"It's a wonderful animal," says the skipper, "and now all of you have seen a sea-serpent; but I forbid any man here to say a word about it when we get ashore."

'"Why not, sir?" says the second mate.

'"Because you wouldn't be believed," said the skipper sternly. "You might all go ashore and make affidavits and not a soul would believe you. The comic papers would make fun of it, and the respectable papers would say it was seaweed or gulls."

'"Why not take it to New York with us?" says the first mate suddenly.

'"What?" says the skipper.

'"Feed it every day," says the mate, getting excited, "and bait a couple of shark hooks and keep them ready, together with some wire rope. Get him to follow us as far as he will, and then hook him. We might get him in alive and show him at a sovereign a head. Anyway, we can take in his carcase if we manage it properly."

'"By George! if only we could," says the skipper, getting excited too.

'"We can try," says the mate. "Why, we could have noosed it this morning if we had liked; and if it breaks the lines we must blow its head to pieces with the gun."

'It seemed a most extraordinary thing to try and catch it that way; but the beast was so tame, and stuck so close to us, that it wasn't so ridiculous as it seemed at first.

'After a couple of days nobody minded the animal a bit, for it was about the most nervous thing of its size you ever saw. It hadn't got the soul of a mouse; and one day when the second mate, just for a lark, took the line of the foghorn in his hand and tooted it a bit, it flung up its head in a scared sort of way, and, after backing a bit, turned clean round and bolted.

'I thought the skipper would go mad. He threw over loaves of bread, bits of beef and pork, and scores of biscuits, and by and by, when the brute plucked up heart and came after us again, he fairly beamed with joy. Then he gave orders that nobody was to touch the horn for any reason whatever, not even if there was a fog, or chance of collision, or anything of the kind; and he also gave orders that the bells weren't to be struck, but that the bosun was just to poke his head in the fo'c'sle and call them out instead.

'After three days had passed, and the thing was still following us, everybody was certain of taking it to New York, and I believe if it hadn't been for Joe Cooper the question about the sea-serpent would have been settled long ago. He was the most extraordinarily ugly chap was Joe. He had a perfect cartoon of a face, and he was so delicate-minded and sensitive about it that if a chap only stopped in the street and whistled as he passed, or pointed him out to a friend, he didn't like it. He told me once when I was sympathizing with him, that the only time a woman ever spoke civilly to him was down Poplar way one night, in a fog, and he was so happy about it that they both walked into the canal before he knew where they were.

'On the fourth morning, when we were only about three days from Sandy Hook, the skipper got out of bed the wrong side, and when he went on deck he was ready to snap at anybody, and as luck would have it, as he walked a bit for'ard, he saw Joe sticking his face over the side looking at the serpent.

'"What d'you think you're doing?" shouts the skipper. "What do you mean by it?"

'"Mean by what, sir?" asks Joe.

'"Putting your ugly face over the side of the ship and frightening my sea-serpent!" bellows the skipper. "You know how easily it's scared."

'"Frightening the sea-serpent?" says Joe, trembling all over, and turning very white.

'"If I see that face of yours over the side again, my lad," says the skipper very fiercely, "I'll give it a black eye. Now cut!"

'Joe cut, and the skipper, having worked off some of his ill-temper, went aft again and began to chat with the mate quite pleasantly. I was down below at the time, and didn't know anything about it for hours afterwards, and then I heard it from one of the firemen. He comes up to me very mysteriously and says, "Bill," he says, "you're a pal of Joe's; come down here and see what you can make of him."

'Not knowing what he meant, I followed him below to the

178

engine-room, and there was Joe sitting on a bucket staring wildly in front of him, and two or three of them standing around looking at him with their heads on one side.

'"He's been like that for three hours," says the second engineer in a whisper, "in a sort of daze."

'As he spoke Joe gave a little shudder; "Frighten the sea-serpent!" says he, in horror.

'"It's turned his brain," says one of the fireman, "he keeps saying nothing but that."

'"If only we could make him cry," says the second engineer, who had a brother who was a medical student, "it might save his reason. But how to do it, that's the question."

'"Speak kindly to him, sir," says the fireman. "I'll have a try if you don't mind." He cleared his throat first, and then walked over to Joe and put his hand on his shoulder and said very softly and pitifully:

'"Don't take on, Joe, don't take on, there's many an ugly face hides a good heart."

'Before he could think of anything else to say, Joe ups with his fist and gives him a jab that nearly breaks his ribs. Then he turns his head away and shivers again, and the old dazed look comes back.

'"Joe," I says, shaking him, "Joe!"

'"Frightened the sea-serpent!" whispers Joe, staring.

'"Joe," I says, "Joe. You know me, I'm your pal, Bill."

'"Ay, ay," says Joe, coming round a bit.

'"Come away," I says, "come and get to bed, that's the best place for you."

'I took him by the sleeve, and he gets up quiet and obedient and follows me like a little child. I got him straight into his bunk, and after a time he fell into a soft slumber, and I thought the worst had passed, but I was mistaken. He got up in three hours' time and seemed all right, except that he walked about as though he was thinking very hard about something, and before I could make out what it was he had a fit.

'He was in that fit ten minutes, and he was no sooner out of that one than he was in another. In twenty-four hours he had six full-sized fits, and I'll allow I was fairly puzzled. What pleasure he could find in tumbling down hard and stiff and kicking at everybody and everything I couldn't see. He'd be standing quiet and peacefully one minute, and the next he'd catch hold of the nearest thing to him and have a bad fit, and lie on his back and kick us while we were trying to force open his hands to pat them.

'The other chaps said the skipper's insult had turned his brain, but I wasn't quite so soft, and one time when he was alone, I put it to him.

'"Joe, old man," I says, "you and I have been very good pals."

'"Ay, ay," says he, suspiciously.

'"Joe," I whispers, "what's you're little game?"

'"What d'you mean?" says he, shortly.

'"I mean the fits," says I, looking at him very steadily. "It's no good looking innocent like that, because I saw you chewing soap with my own eyes."

'"Soap," says Joe, in a nasty sneering way, "you wouldn't recognize a piece if you saw it."

'After that I could see there was nothing to be got out of him, and I just kept my eyes open and watched. The skipper didn't worry about his fits, except that he said he wasn't to let the serpent see his face when he was in them for fear of scaring it; and when the mate wanted to leave him out of the watch, he says "No, he might as well have fits while at work as anywhere else."

'We were about twenty-four hours from port, and the serpent was still following us; and at six o'clock in the evening the officers perfected all their arrangements for catching the creature at eight o'clock next morning. To make quite sure of it an extra watch was kept on deck all night to throw it food every half-hour; and when I turned in at ten o'clock that night it was so close I could have reached it with a clothes-prop.

'I think I'd been in bed about half an hour when I was woken by the most infernal row I ever heard. The foghorn was going incessantly, and there was a lot of shouting and running about on deck. It struck us all that the serpent was getting a bit tired of bread, and was misbehaving himself, consequently we just shoved our heads out of the fore-scuttle and listened. All the hullaballoo seemed to be on the bridge, and as we didn't see the serpent there we plucked up courage and went on deck.

'Then we saw what had happened. Joe had had another fit while at the wheel, and, *not knowing what he was doing*, had clutched the line of the foghorn, and was holding on to it like grim death, and kicking right and left. The skipper was in his nightclothes, raving worse than Joe; and just as we got there Joe came round a bit, and, letting go of the line, asked in a faint voice what the foghorn was blowing for. I thought the skipper was going to kill him; but the second mate held him back, and, of course, when things quietened down a bit, and we went to the side, we found the sea-serpent had vanished.

'We stayed there all that night, but it wasn't any use. When day broke there wasn't the slightest trace of it, and I think the men were as sorry to lose it as the officers. All except Joe, that is, which shows how people should never be rude, even to the humblest; for I'm certain that if the skipper hadn't hurt his feelings the way he did we should now know as much about the sea-serpent as we do about our own brothers.'

Mrs Bunker's Chaperon

MATILDA stood at the open door of a house attached to a wharf situated in that dreary district which bears the high-sounding name of 'St Katherine's'.

Work was over for the day. A couple of unhorsed vans were pushed up the gangway by the side of the house, and the big gate was closed. The untidy office which occupied the ground floor was deserted, except for a grey-bearded 'housemaid' of sixty, who was sweeping it through with a broom, and indulging in a few sailorly oaths at the choking qualities of the dust he was raising.

The sound of advancing footsteps stopped at the gate, a small flap-door let in it flew open, and Matilda Bunker's open countenance took a pinkish hue, as a small man in jersey and blue coat, with a hard round hat exceedingly high in the crown, stepped inside.

'Good evening, Mrs Bunker, ma'am,' said he, coming slowly up to her.

'Good evening, captain,' said the lady, who was Mrs only by virtue of her age and presence.

'Fresh breeze,' said the man in the high round hat. 'If this lasts we'll be in Ipswich in no time.'

Mrs Bunker assented.

'Beautiful the river is at present,' continued the captain. 'Everything growing splendidly.'

'In the river?' asked the mystified Mrs Bunker.

'On the banks,' said the captain; 'the trees, by Sheppey, and all round there. Now, why don't you say the word, and come? There's a cabin like a new pin ready for you to sit in—for cleanness, I mean—and every accommodation you could require. Sleep like a humming-top you will, if you come.'

'Humming-top?' queried Mrs Bunker archly.

'Any top,' said the captain. 'Come, make up your mind. We shan't sail before nine.'

'It doesn't look right,' said the lady, who was sorely tempted. 'But the mistress says I may go if I like, so I'll just go and get my box ready. I'll be down on the jetty at nine.'

'Ay, ay,' said the skipper, smiling. 'Bill and I'll just have a snooze until then. So long.'

'So long,' said Matilda.

'So long,' repeated the amorous skipper, and turning round to bestow another ardent glance upon the fair one at the door, crashed into the wagon.

The neighbouring clocks were just striking nine in a sort of yelping chorus to the heavy boom of Big Ben, which came floating down the river, as Mrs Bunker and the night-watchman, staggering under a load of luggage, slowly made their way on to the jetty. The barge, for such was the craft in question, was almost level with the planks, while the figures of of two men darted to and fro in all the bustle of getting under way.

'Bill,' said the watchman, addressing the mate, 'bear a hand with this box, and be careful, it's got the wedding clothes inside.'

The watchman was so particularly pleased with this little joke that in place of giving the box to Bill he put it down and sat on it, shaking convulsively with his hand over his mouth, while the blushing Matilda and the discomfited captain strove in vain to appear unconcerned.

The packages were rather a tight squeeze for the cabin, but they managed to get them in, and the skipper, with a threatening look at his mate, who was exchanging glances of exquisite humour with the watchman, gave his hand to Mrs Bunker and helped her aboard.

'Welcome on the *Sir Edmund Lyons*, Mrs Bunker,' said he. 'Bill, send that dog back.'

'Stop!' said Mrs Bunker hastily, 'that's my chaperon.'

'Your what?' said the skipper. 'It's a dog, Mrs Bunker, and I won't have any dogs aboard my craft.'

'Bill,' said Mrs Bunker, 'fetch my box up again.'

'Leastways,' the captain hastened to add, 'unless it's any friend of yours, Mrs Bunker.'

'It's chaperoning me,' said Matilda; 'it wouldn't be proper for a lady to go on a voyage with two men without somebody to look after her.'

'That's right, Sam,' said the watchman sententiously. 'You ought to know that at your age.'

'Why, we're looking after her,' said the simple-minded captain. 'Bill and me.'

'Take care Bill doesn't cut you out,' said the watchman in a hoarse whisper, distinctly audible to all. 'He's younger than you are, Sam, and the women are just crazy over young men. Besides which, he's a finer man altogether. And you've had *one* wife already, Sam.'

'Cast off!' said the skipper impatiently. 'Cast off! Stand by there, Bill!'

'Ay, ay!' said Bill, seizing a boat-hook, and the lines fell into the water with a splash as the barge was pushed out into the tide.

Mrs Bunker experienced the usual trouble of landsmen aboard ship, and felt herself terribly in the way as the skipper divided his attentions between the tiller and helping Bill with the sail. Meantime the barge had bothered most of the traffic by laying across the river, and when the sail was hoisted had got under the lee of a huge warehouse and scarcely moved.

'We'll feel the breeze directly,' said Captain Codd. 'Then you'll see what she can do.'

As he spoke, the barge began to slip through the water as a light breeze took her huge sail and carried her into the stream, where she fell into line with other craft who were just making a start.

At a pleasant pace, with wind and tide, the *Sir Edmund Lyons* proceeded on its way, her skipper cocking his eye aloft and along her decks to point out various beauties to his passenger which she might otherwise have overlooked. A comfortable supper was spread on the deck, and Mrs Bunker began to think regretfully of the pleasure she had missed in taking up barge-sailing so late in life.

Greenwich, with its white-fronted hospital and background of trees, was passed. The air got sensibly cooler, and to Mrs Bunker it seemed that the water was not only getting darker, but also lumpy, and she asked two or three times whether there was any danger.

The skipper laughed gaily, and diving down into the cabin fetched up a shawl, which he placed carefully round his fair companion's shoulders. His right hand grasped the tiller, his left stole softly and carefully round her waist.

'How enjoyable!' said Mrs Bunker, referring to the evening.

'Glad you like it,' said the skipper, who wasn't. 'Oh, how pleasant to go sailing down the river of life like this, everything quiet and peaceful, just drifting——'

'Ahoy!' yelled the mate suddenly from the bows. 'Who's steering? Starboard your helm.'

The skipper started guiltily, and put his helm to starboard as another barge came up suddenly from the opposite direction and almost grazed them. There were two men on board, and the skipper blushed for their fluency as reflecting upon the order in general.

It was some little time before they could settle down again after this, but ultimately they got back in their old position, and the infatuated Codd was just about to wax sentimental again, when he felt something behind him. He turned with a start as a portly retriever inserted his head under his left arm, and slowly but vigorously forced himself between them; then he sat on his haunches and panted, while the disconcerted Codd strove to realize the humour of the position.

'I think I shall go to bed now,' said Mrs Bunker, after the position had lasted long enough to be unendurable. 'If anything happens, a collision or anything, don't be afraid to let me know.'

The skipper promised, and, shaking hands, bade his passenger good night. She descended, somewhat clumsily, it is true, into the little cabin, and the skipper, sitting by the helm, which he lazily manœuvred as required, smoked his short clay pipe and fell into a lover's reverie.

So he sat and smoked until the barge, which had, by the help of the breeze, been making its way against the tide, began to realize that that good friend had almost dropped, and at the same time bethought itself of a small anchor which hung over the bows ready for emergencies such as these.

'We must bring up, Bill,' said the skipper.

'Ay, ay!' said Bill, sleepily raising himself from the hatchway. 'Over she goes.'

With no more ceremony than this he dropped the anchor; the sail, with two strong men hauling on to it, creaked and rustled its way close to the mast, and the *Sir Edmund Lyons* was ready for sleep.

'I can do with a nap,' said Bill. 'I'm dog-tired.'

'So am I,' said the other. 'It'll be a tight fit down for'ard, but we couldn't ask a lady to sleep there.'

Bill gave a non-committal grunt, and as the captain, after the manner of his kind, took a last look round before retiring, placed his hands on the hatch and lowered himself down. The next moment he came up with a wild yell, and, sitting on the deck, rolled up his trousers and fondled his leg.

'What's the matter?' inquired the skipper.

'That wretched dog's down there, that's all,' said the injured Bill. 'He's evidently mistaken it for his kennel, and I don't wonder at it. I thought he'd been wonderfully quiet.'

'We must talk him over,' said the skipper, advancing to the hatchway. 'Poor dog! Poor old chap! Come along, then! Come along!' He patted his leg and whistled, and the dog, which wanted to get to sleep again, growled like a small thunderstorm.

'Come on, old fellow!' said the skipper, enticingly. 'Come along, come on, then!'

The dog came at last, and then the skipper, instead of staying to pat him, raced Bill up the ropes, while the brute, in execrable taste, paced up and down the deck daring them to come down.

Coming to the conclusion, at last, that they were settled for the night, he returned to the forecastle and, after a warning bark or two, turned in again. Both men, after waiting a few minutes, cautiously regained the deck.

'You call him up again,' said Bill, seizing a boat-hook, and holding it at the charge.

'Certainly not,' said the other. 'I won't have any blood spilt aboard my ship.'

'Who's going to spill blood?' asked Bill; 'but if he likes to run himself on to the boat-hook——'

'Put it down,' said the skipper sternly, and Bill sullenly obeyed.

'We'll have to snooze on deck,' said Codd.

'And mind we don't snore,' said the sarcastic Bill, '' 'cos the dog mightn't like it.'

Without noticing this remark the captain stretched himself on the hatches, and Bill, after a few more grumbles, followed his example, and both men were soon asleep.

Day was breaking when they awoke and stretched their stiffened limbs, for the air was fresh, with a suspicion of moisture in it. Two or three small craft were, like themselves, riding at anchor, their decks wet and deserted; others were getting under way to take advantage of the tide, which had just turned.

'Up with the anchor,' said the skipper, seizing a handspike and thrusting it into the windlass.

As the rusty chain came in, an ominous growling came from below, and Bill snatched his handspike out and raised it aloft. The skipper gazed meditatively at the shore, and the dog, as it came bounding up, gazed meditatively at the handspike. Then it yawned, an easy, unconcerned yawn, and commenced to pace the deck, and coming to the conclusion that the men were only engaged in necessary work, regarded their efforts with a lenient eye, and barked encouragingly as they hoisted the sail.

It was a beautiful morning. The miniature river waves broke against the blunt bows of the barge, and passed by her sides rippling musically. Over the flat Essex marshes a white mist was slowly dispersing before the rays of the sun, and the trees on the Kentish hills were black and drenched with moisture.

A little later smoke issued from the tiny cowl over the fo'c'sle, and rolled in a little pungent cloud to the Kentish shore. Then a delicious odour of frying steak rose from below, and fell like healing balm upon the susceptible nostrils of the skipper as he stood at the helm.

'Is Mrs Bunker getting up?' inquired the mate, as he emerged from the fo'c'sle and walked aft.

'I believe so,' said the skipper. 'There's movement below.'

'Because the steak's ready and waiting,' said the mate. 'I've put it on a dish in front of the fire.'

188

'Ay, ay!' said the skipper.

The mate lit his pipe and sat down on the hatchway, slowly smoking. He removed it a couple of minutes later, to stare in bewilderment at the unwonted behaviour of the dog, which came up to the captain and affectionately licked his hands.

'He's taken quite a fancy to me,' said the delighted man.

'Love me, love my dog,' quoted Bill waggishly, as he strolled forward again.

The skipper was fondly punching the dog, which was now on its back with its four legs in the air, when he heard a terrible cry from the fo'c'sle, and the mate came rushing wildly on deck.

'Where's that thundering dog?' he cried.

'Don't you talk like that; where's your manners?' cried the skipper.

'Never mind my manners,' said the mate, with tears in his eyes. 'Where's the dog's manners? He's eaten all that steak.'

Before the other could reply, the scuttle over the cabin was drawn, and the radiant face of Mrs Bunker appeared at the opening.

'I can smell breakfast,' said she archly.

'No wonder, with that dog so close,' said Bill grimly.

Mrs Bunker looked at the captain for an explanation.

'He's eaten it,' said that gentleman briefly. 'A pound and a half of the best rump steak in Wapping.'

'Never mind,' said Mrs Bunker sweetly, 'cook some more. I can wait.'

'Cook some more,' said the skipper to the mate, who still lingered.

'I'll cook some bloaters. That's all we've got now,' replied the mate sulkily.

'It's a lovely morning,' said Mrs Bunker, as the mate retired, 'the air is so fresh. I expect that's what has made Rover so hungry. He isn't a greedy dog. Not at all.'

'Very likely,' said Codd, as the dog rose, and, after sniffing the air, gently wagged his tail and trotted forward. 'Where's he off to now?'

'He can smell the bloaters, I expect,' said Mrs Bunker, laughing. 'It's wonderful what intelligence he's got. Come here, Rover!'

'Bill!' cried the skipper warningly, as the dog continued on his way. 'Look out! He's coming!'

'Call him off!' yelled the mate anxiously. 'Call him off!'

Mrs Bunker ran up, and, seizing her chaperon by the collar hauled him away.

'It's the sea air,' she said apologetically; 'and he's been on short commons lately, because he's not been well. Keep still, Rover!'

'Keep still, Rover!' said the skipper, with an air of command.

Under this joint control the dog sat down, his tongue lolling out, and his eyes fixed on the fo'c'sle until the breakfast was spread. The appearance of the mate with a dish of steaming fish excited him again, and being scolded by his mistress, he sat down sulkily in the skipper's plate, until pushed off by its indignant owner.

'Soft roe, Bill?' inquired the skipper courteously, after he had served his passenger.

'That's not my plate,' said the mate pointedly, as the skipper helped him.

'Oh! I wasn't noticing,' said the other, reddening.

'I was, though,' said the mate rudely. 'I thought you'd do that. I was waiting for it. I'm not going to eat after animals, if you are.'

The skipper coughed, and, after effecting the desired exchange, proceeded with his breakfast in sombre silence.

The barge was slipping at an easy pace through the water, the sun was bright, and the air cool, and everything pleasant and comfortable, until the chaperon, who had been repeatedly pushed away, broke through the charmed circle which surrounded the food and seized a fish. In the confusion which ensued he fell foul of the tea-kettle, and, dropping his prey, bit the skipper frantically, until driven off by his mistress.

'Naughty boy!' said she, giving him a few slight cuffs. 'Has he hurt you? I must get a bandage for you.'

'A little,' said Codd, looking at his hand, which was bleeding profusely. 'There's a little linen in the locker down below, if you wouldn't mind tearing it up for me.'

Mrs Bunker, giving the dog a final slap, went below, and the two men looked at each other and then at the dog, which was standing at the stern, barking insultingly at a passing steamer.

'It's about time she came over,' said the mate, throwing a glance at the sail, then at the skipper, then at the dog.

'So it is,' said the skipper, through his set teeth.

As he spoke he pushed the long tiller hastily from port to starboard, and the dog finished his bark in the water; the huge sail reeled for a moment, then swung violently over to the other side, and the barge was on a fresh tack, with the dog twenty yards astern. He was wise in his generation, and after one look at the barge, made for the distant shore.

'Murderers!' screamed a voice; 'murderers! You've killed my dog.'

'It was an accident; I didn't see him,' stammered the skipper.

'Don't tell me,' stormed the lady; 'I saw it all through the skylight.'

'We had to shift the helm to get out of the way of a schooner,' said Codd.

'Where's the schooner?' demanded Mrs Bunker; 'where is it?'

The captain looked at the mate. 'Where's the schooner?' said he.

'I believe,' said the mate, losing his head entirely at this question, 'I believe we must run her down. I don't see her anywhere.'

Mrs Bunker stamped her foot, and, with a terrible glance at the men, descended to the cabin. From this point of vantage she obstinately refused to budge, and sat in angry seclusion until the vessel reached Ipswich late in the evening. Then she appeared on deck, dressed for walking, and, utterly ignoring the woebegone Codd, stepped ashore, and obtaining a cab for her boxes, drove silently away.

An hour afterwards the mate went to his home, leaving the captain sitting on the lonely deck striving to realize the bitter fact that, so far as the end he had in view was concerned, he had seen the last of Mrs Bunker and the small but happy home in which he had hoped to install her.

A Harbour of Refuge

A WATERMAN'S boat was lying in the river just below Greenwich, the waterman resting on his oars, while his fare, a small, perturbed-looking man in seaman's attire, gazed expectantly up the river.

'There she is!' he cried suddenly, as a small schooner came into view from behind a big steamer. 'Take me alongside.'

'Nice little thing she is too,' said the waterman, watching the other out of the corner of his eye as he bent to his oars. 'Rides the water like a duck. Her cap'n knows a thing or two, I'll bet.'

'He knows watermen's fares,' replied the passenger coldly.

'Look out there!' cried a voice from the schooner, and the mate threw a line which the passenger skilfully caught.

The waterman ceased rowing, and, as his boat came alongside the schooner, held out his hand to his passenger, who had already commenced to scramble up the side, and demanded his fare. It was handed down to him.

'It's all right, then,' said the fare, as he stood on the deck and closed his eyes to the painful language in which the waterman was addressing him. 'Nobody been inquiring for me?'

'Not a soul,' said the mate. 'What's all the row about?'

'Well, you see, it's this way,' said the master of the *Frolic*, dropping his voice. 'I've been taking a little too much notice of a little craft down Battersea way—nice little thing, and she thought I was a single man, d'you see?'

The mate sucked his teeth.

'She introduced me to her brother as a single man,' continued the skipper. 'He asked me when the banns were to be put up, and I didn't like to tell him I was a married man with a family.'

'Why not?' asked the mate.

'He's a prize-fighter,' said the other, in awe-inspiring tones; 'the "Battersea Bruiser". Consequently when he clapped me on the back, and asked me when the banns were to be, I only smiled.'

'What did he do?' inquired the mate, who was becoming interested.

'Put them up,' groaned the skipper, 'and we all went to church to hear them. Talk of people walking over your grave, George, it's nothing to what I felt—nothing. I felt a hypocrite, almost. Somehow he found out about me, and I've been hiding ever since I sent you that note. He told a pal he was going to give me a licking, and come down to Fairhaven with us and make mischief between me and the wife.'

'That would be worse than the licking,' said the mate sagely.

'Ah! and she'd believe him before she would me, too, and we've been married seventeen years,' said the skipper mournfully.

'Perhaps that's——' began the mate, and stopped suddenly.

'Perhaps what?' inquired the other, after waiting a reasonable time for him to finish.

'H'm, I've forgotten what I was going to say,' said the mate. 'Funny, it's gone now. Well, you're all right now. You'd intended this to be the last trip to London for some time.'

'Yes, that's what made me a bit more attentive than I should have been,' mused the skipper. 'However, all's well that ends well. How did you get on about the cook? Did you ship one?'

'Yes, I've got one, but he's only signed as far as Fairhaven,' replied the mate. 'Fine strong chap he is. He's too good for a cook. I never saw a better built man in my life. It'll do your eyes good to look at him. Here, cook!'

At the summons a huge, close-cropped head was thrust out of the galley, and a man of beautiful muscular development stepped out before the eyes of the paralysed skipper, and began to remove his coat.

'Isn't he a fine chap?' said the mate admiringly. 'Show him your biceps, cook.'

With a leer at the captain, the cook complied. He then doubled his fists, and, ducking his head scientifically, danced all round the stupefied master of the *Frolic*.

'Put your hands up,' he cried warningly. 'I'm going to hit you!'

'What the dickens are you up to, cook?' demanded the mate, who had been watching his proceedings in speechless amazement.

'Cook!' said the person addressed, with majestic scorn. 'I'm no cook; I'm Bill Simmons, the "Battersea Bruiser", and I shipped on this little tub all for your dear captain's sake. I'm going to put such a head on him that when he wants to blow his nose he'll have to get a looking-glass to see where to go. I'm going to give him a licking every day, and when we get to Fairhaven I'm going to follow him home and tell his wife about him walking out with my sister.'

'She walked me out,' said the skipper, with dry lips.

'Put 'em up,' vociferated the 'Bruiser'.

'Don't you touch me, my lad,' said the skipper, dodging behind the wheel. 'Go and see about your work — go and peel the potatoes.'

'What!' roared the 'Bruiser'.

'You've shipped as cook aboard my craft,' said the skipper

impressively. 'If you lay a finger on me it's mutiny, and you'll get twelve months.'

'That's right,' said the mate, as the pugilist (who had once had fourteen days for bruising, and still held it in wholesome remembrance) paused irresolute. 'It's mutiny, and it'll be my painful duty to get up the shotgun and blow the top of your ugly head off.'

'Would it be mutiny if I was to dot *you* one?' inquired the 'Bruiser', in a voice husky with emotion, as he sidled up to the mate.

'It would,' said the other hastily.

'Well, you're a nice lot,' said the disgusted 'Bruiser', 'you and your mutinies. Will any one of you have a go at me?'

There was no response from the crew, who had gathered round, and were watching the proceedings with keen enjoyment.

'Or all of you?' asked the 'Bruiser', raising his eyebrows.

'I've got no quarrel with you, my lad,' the boy remarked with dignity, as he caught the new cook's eye.

'Go and cook the dinner,' said the skipper; 'and look sharp about it. I don't want to have to find fault with a young beginner like you; but I won't have any shirkers aboard— understand that.'

For one moment of terrible suspense the skipper's life hung in the balance, then the 'Bruiser', restraining his natural instincts by a mighty effort, retreated, growling, to the galley.

The skipper's breath came more freely.

'He doesn't know your address, I suppose,' said the mate.

'No, but he'll soon find it out when we get ashore,' said the other dolefully. 'When I think that I've got to take that brute to my home to make mischief I feel almost tempted to throw him overboard.'

'It is a temptation,' agreed the mate loyally, closing his eyes to his chief's physical deficiencies. 'I'll pass the word to the crew not to let him know your address, anyhow.'

The morning passed quietly, the skipper striving to look unconcerned as the new cook grimly brought the dinner down to the cabin and set it before him. After toying with it a little while, the master of the *Frolic* dined off buttered biscuit.

It was a matter of much discomfort to the crew that the new cook took his duties very seriously, and prided himself on his cooking. He was, moreover, disposed to be inconveniently punctilious about the way in which his efforts were regarded. For the first day the crew ate in silence, but at dinner-time on the second the storm broke.

'What are you looking at your vittles like that for?' inquired the 'Bruiser' of Sam Dowse, as that able-bodied seaman sat with his plate in his lap, eyeing it with much disfavour. 'That isn't the way to look at your food, after I've been perspiring away all the morning cooking it.'

'Yes, you've cooked yourself instead of the meat,' said Sam warmly. 'It's a shame to spoil good food like that; it's quite raw.'

'You eat it!' said the 'Bruiser' fiercely; 'that's what you've got to do. Eat it!'

For sole answer the indignant Sam threw a piece at him, and the rest of the crew, snatching up their dinners, hurriedly clambered into their bunks and viewed the fray from a safe distance.

'Have you had enough?' inquired the 'Bruiser', addressing the head of Sam, which protruded from beneath his left arm.

'I have,' said Sam surlily.

'And you won't turn up your nose at good vittles any more?' inquired the 'Bruiser' severely.

'I won't turn it up at anything,' said Sam earnestly, as he tenderly felt the member in question.

'You're the only one who has complained,' said the 'Bruiser'. 'You're dainty, that's what you are. Look at the others—look how they're eating theirs!'

At this hint the others came out of their bunks and fell to, and the 'Bruiser' became affable.

'It's wonderful what I can turn my hand to,' he remarked pleasantly. 'Things come natural to me that other men have to learn. You'd better put a bit of raw beef on that eye of yours, Sam.'

The thoughtless Sam clapped on a piece from his plate, and it was only by the active intercession of the rest of the crew that the sensitive cook was prevented from inflicting more punishment.

From this time forth the 'Bruiser' ruled the roost, and, his temper soured by his trials, ruled it with a rod of iron. The crew, with the exception of Dowse, were small men getting on in years, and quite unable to cope with him. His attitude with the skipper was dangerously deferential, and the latter was sorely perplexed to think of a way out of the mess in which he found himself.

'He means business, George,' he said one day to the mate, as he saw the 'Bruiser' watching him intently from the galley.

'He looks at you worse and worse,' was the mate's cheering reply. 'The cooking's spoiling what little temper he's got left as fast as possible.'

'It's the scandal I'm thinking of,' groaned the skipper; 'all because I like to be a bit pleasant to people.'

'You mustn't look at the black side of things,' said the mate; 'perhaps you won't need to worry about that after he's hit you. I'd sooner be kicked by a horse myself. He was telling them down for'ard the other night that he killed a chap once.'

The skipper turned green. 'He ought to have been hung for it,' he said vehemently. 'I wonder what juries think they're for in this country. If I'd been on the jury I'd have had my way, if they'd starved me for a month!'

'Look here!' said the mate suddenly; 'I've got an idea. You go down below and I'll call him up and start rating him. When I'm in the thick of it you come and stick up for him.'

'George,' said the skipper, with glistening eyes, 'you're a wonder. Lay it on thick, and if he hits you I'll make it up to you in some way.'

He went below, and the mate, after waiting for some time, leaned over the wheel and shouted for the cook.

'What do you want?' growled the 'Bruiser', as he thrust a visage all red and streaky with his work from the galley.

'Why the devil don't you wash those saucepans up?' demanded the mate, pointing to a row which stood on the deck. 'Do you think we shipped you because we wanted a broken-nosed tenth-rate prize-fighter to look at?'

'Tenth-rate!' roared the 'Bruiser', coming out on to the deck.

'Don't you roar at your officer,' said the mate sternly. 'Your manners are worse than your cooking. You'd better stay with us a few trips to improve them.'

The 'Bruiser' turned purple, and shivered with impotent wrath.

'We get a parcel of loafers aboard here,' continued the mate airily addressing the atmosphere, 'and blow me if they don't think they're here to be waited on. You'll want me to wash your face for you next, and do all your other dirty work, you——'

'George!' said a sad, reproving voice.

The mate started dramatically as the skipper appeared at the companion, and stopped abruptly.

'For shame, George!' said the skipper. 'I never expected to hear you talk to anybody like that, especially to my friend Mr Simmons.'

'Your *what*?' demanded the friend hotly.

'My friend,' repeated the other gently; 'and as to tenth-rate prize-fighters, George, the "Battersea Bruiser" might be champion of England, if he'd only take the trouble to train.'

'Oh, you're always sticking up for him,' said the artful mate.

'He deserves it,' said the skipper warmly. 'He's always run straight, has Bill Simmons, and when I hear him being talked at like that, it makes me go hot all over.'

'Don't you take the trouble to go hot all over on my account,' said the 'Bruiser' politely.

'I can't help my feelings, Bill,' said the skipper softly.

'And don't you call me Bill,' roared the 'Bruiser' with sudden ferocity. 'D'you think I mind what you and your little tinpot crew say. You wait till we get ashore, my friend, and the mate too. Both of you wait!'

He turned his back on them and walked off to the galley, from which, with a view of giving them an object-lesson of an entertaining kind, he presently emerged with a small sack of potatoes, which he slung from the boom and used as a punching ball, dealing blows which made the master of the *Frolic* sick with apprehension.

'It's no good,' he said to the mate; 'kindness is thrown away on that man.'

'Well, if he hits one, he's got to hit the lot,' said the mate. 'We'll stand by you.'

'I can't always have the crew following me about,' said the skipper dejectedly. 'No, he'll wait his opportunity, and, after he's broken my head, he'll go home and break my wife's heart.'

'She won't break her heart,' said the mate confidently. 'She and you will both have a rough time of it; perhaps it would be better for you if she did break it a bit, but she's not that sort of woman. Well, those of us who live longest'll see the most.'

For the remainder of that day the cook maintained a sort of unnatural calm. The *Frolic* rose and fell on the seas like a cork, and the 'Bruiser' took short unpremeditated little runs about the deck, which aggravated him exceedingly. Between the runs he folded his arms on the side, and languidly cursed the sea and all that belonged to it; and finally, having lost all desire for food himself, went below and turned in.

He stayed in his bunk the whole of the next day and night, awaking early the following morning to the pleasant fact that the motion had ceased, and that the sides and floor of the fo'c'sle were in the places where people of regular habits would expect to find them. The other bunks were empty, and, after a toilet hastened by a yearning for nourishment, he ran up on deck.

Day had just broken, and he found to his surprise that the voyage was over, and the schooner in a small harbour, lying alongside a stone quay. A few unloaded trucks stood on a railway line which ran from the harbour to the town clustered behind it, but there was no sign of work or life; the good people of the place evidently being comfortably in their beds, and in no hurry to quit them.

The 'Bruiser', with a happy smile on his face, surveyed the scene, sniffing with joy the smell of the land as it came fresh and sweet from the hills at the back of the town. There was only one thing wanting to complete his happiness—the skipper.

'Where's the cap'n?' he demanded of Dowse, who was methodically coiling a line.

'Just gone home,' replied Dowse shortly.

In a great hurry the 'Bruiser' sprang on to the side and stepped ashore, glancing keenly in every direction for his prey. There was no sign of it, and he ran a little way up the road until he saw the approaching figure of a man, from whom he hoped to obtain information. Then, happening to look back, he saw the masts of the schooner gliding by the quay, and, retracing his steps a little, perceived to his intense surprise, the figure of the skipper standing by the wheel.

'Ta, ta, cookie!' cried the skipper cheerily.

Angry and puzzled the 'Bruiser' ran back to the edge of the quay, and stood owlishly regarding the schooner and the grinning faces of its crew as they hoisted the sails and slowly swung around with their bow pointing to the sea.

'Well, they aren't making a long stay, old man,' said a voice at his elbow, as the man for whom he had been waiting came up. 'Why, they only came in ten minutes ago. What did they come for, do you know?'

'They belong here,' said the 'Bruiser'; 'but me and the skipper's had words, and I'm waiting for him.'

'That craft doesn't belong here,' said the stranger, as he eyed the receding *Frolic*.

'Yes, it does,' said the 'Bruiser'.

'I tell you it doesn't,' said the other. 'I ought to know.'

'Look here, my friend,' said the 'Bruiser' grimly, 'don't contradict me. That's the *Frolic* of Fairhaven.'

'Very likely,' said the man. 'I don't know where she's from, but she's not from here.'

'Why,' said the 'Bruiser', and his voice shook, 'isn't this Fairhaven?'

'Good gracious, no!' said the stranger; 'not by a couple of hundred miles it isn't. What put that idea into your silly fat head?'

The frantic 'Bruiser' raised his fist at the description, but at that moment the crew of the *Frolic*, which was just getting clear of the harbour, hung over the stern and gave three hearty cheers. The stranger was of a friendly and excitable disposition, and, his evil star being in the ascendant that morning, he took off his hat and cheered wildly back. Immediately afterwards he obtained unasked the post of whipping-boy to the master of the *Frolic*, and entered upon his new duties at once.